Am T.C.F. Na

The
Regulator

*Also by Ray Hogan
in Large Print:*

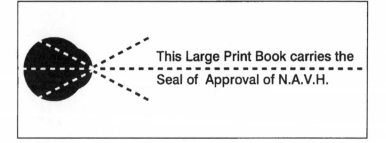

The Regulator

The Life and Death of William Thompson

Ray Hogan

Thorndike Press • Waterville, Maine

The characters in this book, except for the principal one, William Thompson, are fictitious, and any resemblance to persons living or dead is purely coincidental.

Published in 2005 by arrangement with Golden West Literary Agency.

Thorndike Press® Large Print Western.

The tree indicium is a trademark of Thorndike Press.

The text of this Large Print edition is unabridged.
Other aspects of the book may vary from the original edition.

Set in 16 pt. Plantin by Christina S. Huff.

Printed in the United States on permanent paper.

Library of Congress Cataloging-in-Publication Data

Hogan, Ray, 1908–
    The regulator : the life and death of William Thompson / by Ray Hogan.
      p. cm. — (Thorndike Press large print Western)
    ISBN 0-7862-7400-X (lg. print : hc : alk. paper)
    1. Oklahoma — Fiction. 2. Cattle stealing — Fiction.
3. Western stories. 4. Large type books. I. Title.
II. Thorndike Press large print Western series.
PS3558.O3473R394 2005
  813′.54—dc22   2004027829

The Regulator

As the Founder/CEO of NAVH, the only national health agency solely devoted to those who, although not totally blind, have an eye disease which could lead to serious visual impairment, I am pleased to recognize Thorndike Press* as one of the leading publishers in the large print field.

Founded in 1954 in San Francisco to prepare large print textbooks for partially seeing children, NAVH became the pioneer and standard setting agency in the preparation of large type.

Today, those publishers who meet our standards carry the prestigious "Seal of Approval" indicating high quality large print. We are delighted that Thorndike Press is one of the publishers whose titles meet these standards. We are also pleased to recognize the significant contribution Thorndike Press is making in this important and growing field.

Lorraine H. Marchi, L.H.D.
Founder/CEO
NAVH

* Thorndike Press encompasses the following imprints: Thorndike, Wheeler, Walker and Large Print Press.

Foreword

No claim is made to the absolute veracity of this book. Because so few facts are known about William Thompson, surmise must be irretrievably linked with the scattering of truths available.

In the beginning I wondered if I were dealing with nothing more than a myth. Had I undertaken to delineate the life and death of one of those nebulous characters of the early West who appear abruptly out of nowhere and, with guns blazing, soar across the horizon like brilliant stars to disappear as suddenly into oblivion leaving little, if anything, to mark their passage?

But Bill Thompson was a flesh-and-blood man despite the lack of records to note either his birth or his death. Such is not unusual, and is explainable. Colorado, where he was slain, filed no death certificates until 1900, and his birth, as so often was the case with early-day individuals, is totally shrouded in obscurity. Only one man, A. W. Thompson (no relation), made note of encountering the legendary range detective — in his book *Those Were Open Range Days* — and there is no reason to doubt Thompson, who was an able and reliable journalist.

Accordingly, the events chronicled in this biography are factual to the best of my knowledge. Invention and conjecture have been employed to make a smoother, more readable narrative.

RAY HOGAN

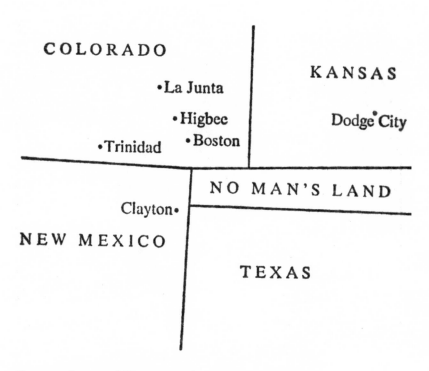

Location of Boston is approximate (no trace of town remains)
Scale: 1/2" approximately 50 miles

1

Thompson, crouched in the low brush on the rim of a bluff, looked down into the arroyo below where the outlaws had disappeared. The maze of mesquite, ironwood, rabbit brush, and other weedy growth combined with the gravelly soil should make it near impossible to pick up the trail left by the men, but there it was — plain as wet cat tracks on a dry rock . . . too plain.

Thompson shifted, drew back from the irregular edge of the cut. Taking a red bandanna from a hip pocket, he mopped at his round, florid face and moodily considered the steel-blue sky beyond the tills. He had been tracking the Boswell brothers for days — and they knew it.

Caught cold-turkey rustling stock from a cattleman named Carpenter, they had managed to escape both the rancher's cowhands and the sheriff, who had given chase; and since the Boswells — Pete, Dade, and Gid — were known to be making a practice of helping themselves regularly not only to

Carpenter beef but to that of other cattle growers as well, a decision was made finally to do something about it, and Thompson was called in.

Carpenter and his fellow ranchers had then relaxed, confident their troubles with rustlers would soon be over: William Thompson, the Regulator, was on the job, and he had a reputation for never failing. One of those hard-eyed, iron-jawed, deadly men known as range detectives who walked the thin line between legal and illegal, he had the wary respect of lawless and law-abiding alike.

Coming to his feet, Thompson walked slowly to where he had picketed his horse, a big, barrel-chested buckskin. Again he mopped at his sweaty brow. Stocky, thick-shouldered, he was somewhat on the heavy side, had sandy-brown hair, a full moustache, and black, overhanging brows.

Dressed in cord pants, low-heeled Hyer boots, flannel shirt, and worn leather vest, he topped off his accouterments with a narrow-brimmed, high-crowned hat pinched to a peak. A Colt forty-five single-action pistol was strapped about his ample waist, and the belt that held it and its well-oiled holster in place gleamed with a full row of brass cartridges.

Halting beside the buckskin, Thompson threw a glance at the sun. Almost noon. It would get hotter and he'd as soon have the matter of the Boswell brothers over and done with before the middle of the afternoon, when the heat reached its peak. Like all men inclining to overweight, he was never comfortable when the temperature was high.

Swinging onto the saddle, the Regulator sat for a few moments studying the land to the south. The arroyo appeared to curve, to cut back toward itself in a wide loop. At its sharpest point was where he'd find the Boswells, sitting there guns ready, waiting in ambush for him to come down the sandy trace following the trail they had left for him. A bleak smile pulled down the corners of his mouth; the damned fools should know better than to think he'd fall for a greenhorn trick.

Wheeling the buckskin gelding about, he doubled back for a distance and then, pointing due west, rode through the dense brush for a good quarter mile. There, changing course again, he headed his horse once more for the deep wash but this time angling for the area below the bend.

Drawing near, Thompson slowed, tested the faint breeze. He grunted his satisfaction. It was in his face. Any sounds of approach would not be heard by the outlaws. Continuing, he moved in nearer to the arroyo, halted finally in a thick stand of twisted mesquite.

Calm, as indifferent as if he were pulling up in front of a general store in some settlement where he intended to enter and buy trail grub and other supplies, Thompson dismounted, looped the buckskin's reins about a stout limb, and making only one concession to the prospect of facing three dangerous outlaws by lifting the weapon on his hip slightly to be certain it would clear the holster easily, he started for the wash.

A stride or two short of the cut, Bill Thompson bent low and, hat off and in his left hand, worked his way quietly through the brush until he was close to the rim of the wash. Dropping flat, he stretched out full-length and wormed his way forward to where he could look down into the arroyo. Again a hard half smile broke the stolidness of his features. The Boswells were there — waiting — just as he had anticipated.

Pete, the eldest of the three according to the description given to him earlier, was perched on a rock at the far side of the bend. The outlaw was well hidden from sight of anyone coming down the wash by a bulge of weed-studded red earth. Directly opposite him were Dade and Gid, hunched shoulder to shoulder behind a screen of tangled brush. They were all staring up the arroyo, eyes fixed on the point where he was expected to appear.

"He ain't coming."

It was either Dade or the youngest of the brothers, Gid, making the comment. Thompson could not be sure which had spoken.

"He'll come," Pete said confidently. "A blind man could follow that trail we left."

"Just what I'm worrying about. Maybe we made it too easy and it's set him to thinking."

Pete swore impatiently, spat. "Keep up that yammering and he sure'n hell won't show up because you'll have scared him off! You just be damn sure you're ready when he does come."

"If'n he does. He could've give up. We ain't for sure he —"

"Bill Thompson ain't the kind that gives up," Pete Boswell said, swiping at the sweat on his dark face. "And that means one thing for certain: we've got to get him or we're done for. He'll dog us till kingdom come if we don't."

"You run up against him before, Pete?"

"Only heard talking about him. A real

15

mean son-of-a-bitch they say, and somebody you sure don't want to trifle with. Don't mind telling you boys I'm a mite jumpy."

"You?"

"Me," Boswell said. "I ain't no fool. This here day's going to end with him dead — or us dead. That's the way he works. With him there just ain't no two ways about it."

"Then why don't we pull out now, keep on going?"

"Because, like I said, we'd never get shut of him, that's why. And we won't ever find a better place than this to have it out with him."

"Could mount up, ride like hell for Montana or maybe Wyoming. Ought to be able to shake him up there."

"Not likely. He'd be on our tails all the way," Pete replied heavily, and then added, "Sure is a tough break. We had things going real good for us down here till they brung him in."

"Should've quit a month ago when we sold off that last bunch of steers in Fort Worth. Had us plenty of cash then."

"Hindsight's always mighty comforting," Pete said dryly, shifting his position, "only it don't never change nothing. We've drawed this hand we're holding, ain't nothing to do now but play it out."

16

"Well, I'm for doing what Gid said," Dade Boswell declared. His voice was lower, firmer. It had been the youngest of the Boswells who had been carrying on the conversation with Pete, Thompson realized. "Let's get the horses and ride the hell out of here. I'd rather take my chances running from this jasper than setting here trying to outfigure him."

Somewhere off in the low hills a gopher barked, the sound high and sharp in the hot, still air. Thompson stirred, watched as Pete Boswell again changed position. The outlaws were getting edgy, the long wait beginning to tell on their nerves.

He would prefer to have them bunched more closely before making his move, but he reckoned it didn't really matter. It would all end the same — in the blasting of guns. Pulling back from the lip of the arroyo, Thompson came upright. Glancing about, he paused, eyes settling on a rider coming in from the west. For a brief time he studied the horseman and then, shrugging, drew his weapon and returned to the rim of the wash.

"Could be you're right, Gid," Pete Boswell was saying. "Might be we ought to line out —"

"Too late, boys," Thompson cut in coldly, his squat figure silhouetted against the sky

17

on the edge of the arroyo slightly behind them. "Your traveling days are over."

Pete sprang to his feet. A wild desperation filled his eyes and his mouth was agape. Gid and Dade Boswell, still crouched, swiveled about, features frozen in shock.

"Drop your guns," Thompson ordered in low, spaced words. "And stand up — slow."

A convulsion of fear tore at Pete Boswell's taut face. Abruptly he threw up his rifle. "You ain't taking me back to no lynching!" he shouted as he leveled the weapon at the range detective. "I'll see you in hell first!"

Thompson's bullet smashing into his chest killed the outlaw before he could squeeze the trigger of the rifle.

Smoothly, swiftly, Bill Thompson swung to the remaining Boswells. Dade fired in that same fragment of time. The slug, aimed hastily, was a clean miss, but the Regulator's accuracy was deadly. Dade Boswell went down, and in the succeeding moment Grid also staggered, went over backward as Thompson's third bullet drove into him before he could get off a shot.

For a long minute Bill Thompson hung motionless there on the rim of the brush-filled arroyo while thin tendrils of powder smoke drifted about his stocky, spread-legged shape, and then stirring, he thumbed open the loading gate of his pistol, rodded out the spent cartridges in its cylinder, and reloaded it. Dropping it back into its holster, he wheeled, moved leisurely toward the buckskin. There was no need to have a look at the outlaws; he knew they were dead.

Reaching the horse, Thompson jerked the lines free and swung onto the saddle. The rider he'd seen coming up from the west had altered course, he noted, was now approaching at a steady lope. He'd heard the gunshots, was intending to investigate.

Cutting the gelding around, Thompson rode to the wash, followed along its edge until he reached a place where the horse could safely descend the steep bank, and dropped down onto the sandy floor of the broad arroyo. Doubling back, he returned to where the Boswell brothers lay. Halting nearby, he dismounted, sought out the outlaws' horses, and led them in to where they would be ready for use.

Methodically collecting the rustlers' weapons and placing them in a pile, Thompson then dragged the Boswells to the center of the wash and laid them out in a row, faceup. He stood for a time after that closely studying the features of each as if he might be searching for a familiar face. Apparently failing in the effort, he began to load the outlaws onto their horses, hanging them across their saddles and securing them with short lengths of rope that he took from his saddlebags.

He had just completed the chore when the thud of hoofs warned him of the arrival of the rider he had noted. Arms folded across his chest, Bill stepped back into the open and awaited the man's appearance on the rim of the wash.

A minute or so elapsed, and then the rider, a young cowhand wearing batwing chaps, was suddenly on the bank above staring down at him.

"What the hell . . ." he began as his eyes fastened on the bodies of the outlaws draped across their saddles.

Thompson, always blunt and to the point, nodded crisply. "Rustlers . . . you know Asa Carpenter?"

The young puncher swallowed hard. "Sure. I work for him. This here's Carpenter range you're on."

"Want you to hunt him up — now. Tell him I've nailed his rustlers and I'll meet him in town, about dark. Understand?"

The cowhand bobbed. "Yes, sir. Who — who'll I say told me?"

"He'll know," Thompson replied, and

abruptly turned away, signifying the end of the conversation.

Gathering the weapons of the outlaws, he stowed the pistols in his saddlebags, returned the rifles to their boots. Then, taking up the reins of the three horses, he linked the animals together pack-string fashion, and holding to the lead horse's lines, mounted the buckskin and struck off down the arroyo.

When he rode up out of the cut a short time later and pointed for the settlement, some fifteen miles distant, the young cowhand he'd sent to summon Carpenter was a small, dark blur disappearing into the south.

2

"That'll be him," the sheriff said, pointing to a faint dust haze east of the settlement where he officiated as the law.

Asa Carpenter, a spare, graying man with thin lips and small, bright eyes, nodded. "Told Wooster he'd be here by dark. I reckon he will."

The lawman crossed his arms, leaned back against the front wall of the jail. "I ain't liking him much," he murmured. "Expect them Boswells never had a chance."

"The association hired him on to get them, Lafe," Carpenter said coldly. "Just what he done."

The sheriff nodded agreement. "Ain't disputing that. Just would've rather he'd brought them in alive and let the law take care of executing them by hanging. This here Regulator fellow never seems to get around to doing it that way, seems. Always hauls them in slung across their saddles."

"One reason, maybe, why he's good at his job. Where'd he ever get that name, the

22

Regulator? Kind of an odd thing to call a man."

Lafe Ryan shook his head. "Heard someone say that he was mixed up in a feud somewheres. One side called themselves the Moderators, other bunch was called the Regulators. Thompson run with them and the handle stuck."

"Couldn't be the reason," Carpenter said. "I recollect that feud. Was back in the forties. Thompson ain't old enough to've been mixed up in that. How long's he been a range detective?"

The lawman's shoulders stirred. "Ain't for sure — and they's a story goes with that, too, just as there is about everything else he's done. It's said that he once had himself a family and a ranch somewheres, and that while he was off driving a herd of cattle to market, a bunch of outlaws rode into his place.

"They just moved in on his woman and kids, took over — was hiding out from the law. They used the woman something awful, and then when they lit out, they burned the place down — with his wife and kids inside. Thompson was supposed to have run into them — there was four in the gang — while he was coming home. Even stopped, passed the time of day with them not knowing they'd come from his place and what they'd done.

"When he did find out, it turned him sort of loony and right off he started hunting them outlaws, made it his business just like he hired out to you and the association to run down the Boswells. Man's got a God-awful hate gnawing at him, so I suspect the story's true. Sure has turned him into the worst kind of a killer."

"What he does is always inside the law," the rancher said defensively.

"Ain't saying it ain't. He's smart and careful when it comes to that, but to my way of thinking he ain't but one notch better'n the outlaws he hunts down — mostly so's he can have a look at them."

Carpenter frowned, brushed at his mouth. "Now, what's that mean?"

Lafe Ryan, gaze on the slowly approaching dust cloud, said, "Folks claim he ain't near as interested in catching outlaws as a range detective as he is in finding them four renegades that murdered his family. Always has himself a good look at whoever he cuts down like he was hoping it'll be one of them four that ruined everything for him."

Carpenter was in deep thought for a long time. Then, "Well, I'd sure hate to be one of them. He'll find them someday and they all better pray he kills them before he recognizes who they are."

"If it's for true in the first place," Ryan said, swiping at the sweat on his forehead with a back of a hand. "Always a lot of tales get started about fellows like Thompson — and a man never knows what to believe. Some little thing happens that maybe don't amount to a tinker's damn, and then before you know it, it gets stretched all out to where it's so big that it gets spread all over the country.

"People are mighty bad about that — blowing up nothing much into something big and making a hero out of whoever it's all about. I don't hold with it."

"But you're admitting that Thompson gets the job done once he's been hired."

"You saying the law don't?"

"Not always. I'll be plain spoken with you, Lafe. You and your deputies had your chance at catching the Boswells a couple of times, and you failed. Took Bill Thompson a little more'n a week."

"We had other things to do," Ryan said stiffly. "Being sheriff calls for me to look out for other folks' troubles, too. Can't just lock up the office and spend all my time running down rustlers."

"Then you hadn't ought to fault Thompson for doing his job."

"Ain't faulting him, only saying —" The sheriff broke off without finishing as if at a loss for words with which to express himself.

Carpenter's severe expression altered slightly into one of dry humor. "Expect you ain't the only lawman that's had to admit Thompson got done what he couldn't."

Ryan made no answer, his attention now fixed on the man with three horses trailing behind him entering the settlement at the far end of the street.

"Have it your way, Asa," he said finally and, pulling himself upright from the wall of the jail, moved to the hitchrack fronting it.

The rancher also turned his attention upon Thompson, now in the center of the dusty roadway and drawing near. People were coming out of the stores and houses edging the sidewalks to stare at the grim procession, but the thickset, slumped man astride the buckskin looked neither right nor left, seemingly unaware of the interest and attention his passage was eliciting.

"Sure looks like anything but what he is," Carpenter said wonderingly, pulling off his hat and running fingers through his iron-gray hair. "Man'd take him for some kind of a drummer if it wasn't for the look on his face."

Lafe Ryan, features a disapproving mask, remained silent, eyes riveted on Thompson. He watched in silence as the detective swung up to the rack, halted, dismounted wearily. He made no move to assist the man as he stepped back to the string of corpse-burdened horses, untied their connecting reins, and tethered each in turn to the crossbar. Thompson, reciprocally, gave him not the slightest note, put his attention on Asa Carpenter.

"There's your rustlers," he said, moving slowly up to the rancher. "Job's done."

Carpenter nodded and, crossing to the horses, had his look at the faces of the dead men. "The Boswells, sure enough," he said, as if there might be some doubt. Reaching into a pocket he produced a small, string-tied leather poke, handed it to Thompson. "Three hundred in double eagles, just as we agreed on. You've done a good job."

Thompson accepted the sack and, unbuttoning his shirt, thrust it inside. "Will you tend to the burying?"

Carpenter nodded. "I'll see to it."

The range detective, his broad face impassive, almost sullen, shifted his attention to Lafe Ryan. "You got anything you want to say to me, Sheriff?"

The lawman's eyes sparked. "Expecting you to bring them in alive's be hoping for too much, I reckon."

"They had their choosings," Thompson replied coolly.

"Seems that's always the story," Ryan countered. "Sure funny to me none of them's ever willing to just give up."

"Well, you worry about it, Sheriff, I don't," Thompson said indifferently. "That all?"

Ryan took a folded bit of paper from his vest pocket. "This here telegram come for you. Was sent to me. I expect they figured I'd know where to find you."

Thompson accepted the bit of paper and, unfolding it, studied the scrawled words. Carpenter watched curiously.

"Bad news?" he asked.

The range detective brushed his hat to the back of his head. Beads of sweat glistened on his ruddy face and there was a tinge of red to his moustache and beard stubble from the trail dust he'd accumulated.

"Nope, just another job. I reckon the sheriff can fill you in."

Ryan flushed angrily at the implication, and then he shrugged. "Matter of fact, I did read it. Didn't have no reason not to. Come from some cattleman up in Clayton, New Mexico Territory. They got the same trouble you've had — rustlers. Offering him a job of cleaning them out."

"You taking it?" the rancher asked.

"Ain't no reason not to," Thompson said. "All finished here."

"How'd they know where you were?" Carpenter continued, eyes on Thompson, who moved to his horse and began to dig into his saddlebags for the outlaws' weapons.

"Word gets around," the detective said laconically, handing the three pistols to Ryan. "Where's the telegraph office?"

Carpenter jerked his thumb in the direction of the stage depot. "Over there. You pulling out right away?"

"Some reason why I shouldn't?" Thompson asked, retracing his steps to the buckskin and swinging up onto the saddle.

The rancher's shoulders lifted, fell. "Nope, no special reason for asking, only I aimed to buy you supper was you going to be around. Can get a mighty fine meal over there at the hotel."

The range detective favored the cattleman with his forced, almost bleak smile. "Obliged to you, but I'll be riding on soon's I send an answer to this fellow McBride in

29

Clayton that I'm on my way. Expect that'll suit the sheriff real fine."

"It will," Ryan said bluntly.

Again a faint grin cracked Thompson's lips. "Always was one to oblige," he said sardonically, and moved on.

3

When Bill Thompson rode into Clayton that late-summer afternoon, the infant settlement was a dusty swirl of activity. Not only had it become an important railhead for the shipping of cattle to eastern markets but it was also experiencing the backwash from the land rush that had taken place earlier that year in adjoining Territory of Oklahoma.

Pulling to a stop at the end of the teeming street, Thompson drew out the telegram that had summoned him to the area. It was signed by a John McBride and instructed him to get in touch with the U.S. deputy marshal when he arrived and from him obtain information as to how he could find the Box M Ranch, where he was to report.

Thompson refolded the sheet of paper, tucked it back into a pocket, and let his small, black eyes drift over the town, thinly veiled by a motionless haze of dust. It was mostly tar-paper shacks and lean-tos with only a few substantial-looking buildings in evidence. Settling his probing gaze on the largest of the numerous saloons, the burly range detective roweled his buckskin horse lightly and began to thread his way through the confusion of traffic for the hitchrack of the establishment.

Reaching the crossbar, he dismounted, tied the gelding securely alongside the dozen or more other patiently waiting horses, and stepping up onto the narrow board landing, entered the noise-filled, hall-like structure. Shouldering a path through the drovers, land-speculators, gamblers, cowhands, and other patrons of the place, he crossed to the bar. No drinker of note, Thompson nevertheless ordered a whiskey. Tossing it off, he paid the stated price of two bits and fixed his implacable attention on the bartender.

"How'll I find the McBride place?"

The sweating, red-faced man behind the counter, wearied by the demands of his job, shook his head impatiently.

"Mister, I ain't got no time to —"

"Take time," Thompson cut in coldly.

The bartender hesitated, his eyes on Thompson's relentless, unforgiving features. He shrugged. "Ten, maybe twelve miles northeast of here."

The range detective eased back, some of the menacing tautness fading from his manner. Nearby patrons had paused, were staring at him curiously, taking in his squat figure, the small, peaked hat, the promise of utter violence that clung to him. A few, apparently recognizing him, were exchanging comments at low voice.

Abruptly, Thompson nodded curtly to the bartender. "Obliged," he said, and wheeling, pushed his way back through the press to the street.

Once more in the open, he halted, again had his look about, debating with himself the advisability of staying the night in Clayton or riding on to McBride's. Drawing a cigar from a metal case carried in a shirt pocket, he bit off the closed end of the weed, fired a match with his thumbnail, and puffed the brown cylinder into life.

There was nothing in Clayton to keep him, he decided. Just as well move on, find McBride, learn what the trouble was and what he was expected to do about it, and get busy. Time on his hands, hours during which he did nothing bored him and was something he studiously avoided. When a man was on the job, he had no time to think of other things, and the memories lurking in the dark recesses of his mind had no chance to creep forward, reopen the old scars, and unleash the consuming hates.

Stepping down off the saloon's landing, Bill walked toward the waiting buckskin, again aware of and ignoring the attention that several persons close by had turned upon him. And then his short, deliberate stride slowed and he came to a halt. His eyes narrowed and his mouth became a thin line. A lawman was standing beside the buckskin waiting for him.

Planting himself squarely on his feet, cigar clenched between his teeth, Thompson considered the lawman — a U.S. deputy marshal, he noted from the badge the man wore. Tall and lank, with a faint droop to his shoulders, he appeared to be somewhere in his early fifties.

"Name's Clevenger," the lawman said, his narrow face expressionless. Reaching up, he hooked a thumb under his star and tipped it forward. "Reckon you can see what I am."

The range detective said nothing, merely watched and waited with an icy disinterest.

"You're Bill Thompson."

The squat, thickset man still made no reply. The crowd surrounding the two was building rapidly and a voice, coming from somewhere in its depths, said, "It's that bird they call the Regulator," as if answering a question put by another bystander.

"I heard the Cattleman's Association had

sent for you," Clevenger said. "Not saying I approve the idea."

A splatter of gunshots broke out beyond the mercantile store, designated as the C & C Company, and for a few moments everyone's interest, including that of Deputy Marshal Clevenger, was turned to that direction. It brought no visible change to the stolid features of the range detective, however. Cigar in a corner of his mouth, he continued to regard the lawman with bland indifference.

"Was saying I don't hold with bringing in your kind," Clevenger resumed after a time. "And I —"

"My kind?" Thompson interrupted coolly, speaking finally. "What's that mean?"

"Gunslingers, that's what," the marshal replied, equally cold. "I got enough problems up here — what with folks pouring in from all over the country — without them sending for the likes of you."

Thompson puffed thoughtfully on his cigar. "Maybe you've got me figured wrong, Marshal. I'm here to do the same thing you're hired for: enforce the law."

"Like hell!" Clevenger snapped. "You're up here to stop the rustling that's going on over on the Strip and thereabouts, and your way of doing it is by killing."

"If I have to. Man gets his chance to throw

down his gun and come along peaceable. He decides against that, it's his funeral."

"Seems when you're there they always decide against it."

Thompson's thick shoulders twitched. "You blame them? They know there's a rope waiting for them and probably figure they've got nothing to lose by trying to outgun me."

"Which they don't ever manage to do."

Again Bill Thompson's shoulders stirred. "Matter of luck, Marshal."

"Luck!" Clevenger snorted. "Why don't you just say it right out? They don't have a chance against you when it comes down to drawing a gun — figuring they get the opportunity to even try —"

Thompson's jaw hardened. "They all get their choice," he said quietly and moved up to the buckskin. "You had your say?"

Clevenger bobbed. "All but this, Thompson: you stay inside the law. Take one step over the line and I'll be after you."

The range detective gave that thought as he pulled the buckskin gelding's lines free of the rack. "Aim to do whatever I'm hired for," he said, swinging onto the saddle. "No more . . . and no less."

"That'd better not include no lawbreaking!" Clevenger said in a rising tone. "I've had reports about you and how you get your job done. I'm warning you right here and now, don't you try no —"

"Expect I'll be doing what I have to do," Bill Thompson said, and cut the buckskin away from the hitchrack.

Immediately the crowd parted, opened an aisle for him. Face wooden, looking neither right nor left, he rode through the lane of gawking bystanders on farther into the street pulsing with pedestrians, heavy-wheeled wagons, dust-filmed buggies, and countless riders on horseback.

Reaching the end of the brief thoroughfare, Thompson glanced at the sun, took his bearings from its position, and pointed the gelding northeast. There was a hard-set smile on his lips. The story was always the same, he thought bitterly; no matter where he went, he was about as welcome, insofar as the law was concerned, as an epidemic of foot-and-mouth disease.

But it never troubled him. His business was to stop rustling and he did it the only way he knew how — with a gun. Generally, the only complaints he had were from the outlaws themselves and from lawmen who resented his being called in.

That was all that bothered Deputy Marshal Clevenger. He had simply been letting off steam and trying to save face in front of the town. Clayton's lawman, too, either a town marshal, or perhaps a sheriff if the settlement was a county seat, would probably unload on him in the same vein when he got the opportunity. It didn't matter. He supposed he couldn't blame any lawmen who had to stand by and see a range detective brought in to stop the lawlessness they had been hired to control but had failed at.

Well, likely he wouldn't be around long enough to give them cause for much irritation. Usually it took only a couple of weeks, possibly a month, to track down a gang of rustlers and put an end to their activities, after which he would follow his usual custom and ride on.

Settling himself on the big, double-rigged saddle, Thompson looked ahead. Ten or twelve miles to the McBride place, the bartender had said. That shouldn't take long.

4

It was a land of many bluffs, rock-studded slopes, and ragged washes floored with fine, white sand. Cottonwood trees grew in the deeper swales and hollows, and dark-trunked cedars and junipers spotted the grassy flats. The Cimarron River, barely up to the buckskin's knees at its deepest, was narrow where he forded it, and the country rolling back from its banks, despite the lateness of the summer, was richly green.

Twice Thompson halted, once in a deep coulee where a spring bubbled out of the earth's depths to form a shallow pool shaded by several spreading cottonwoods, and again on a flinty knoll that overlooked a broad, rough brake. He made mental note of the ragged, bushy area with its countless arroyos and washes; like as not it had afforded sanctuary for many rustlers and other lawbreakers, and he reckoned he could expect to visit it often before the job he was being hired to do was finished.

Well on into the afternoon, following a

slow, easy ride that had given him a fairly good idea of the country he would be covering, the range detective came in sight of the McBride ranch. It was far from impressive: a single house that evidently sheltered the cattleman and his family, a bunkhouse off the end of which the cook maintained his kitchen and dining quarters, a small barn, a scatter of lesser sheds, and several corrals. It was a working ranch, Thompson realized, one devoid of all the unnecessary and designed strictly for raising beef.

Two riders angled across a yucca- and rabbit-brushpocked flat as if to intercept him as he rode toward the cluster of buildings, but he paid them no mind, simply continued on his way, pointing the buckskin for the hitchrack that fronted the largest of the structures.

He had scarcely halted at the crossbar when the door of the house opened and a man stepped out onto the porch, which extended the width of the building. Thompson, nodding briefly, alighted from the saddle. Wrapping the gelding's lines about the rough-hewn pole, he paused, eyes on the smoky-blue mountains in the distant northwest for a moment, and then pivoting, moved for the man waiting on the porch.

"You John McBride?"

The rancher, somewhere in his sixties, balding, ruddy complexioned, and with a testy impatience showing in his dark eyes, nodded vigorously.

"That's me. You Thompson, the one they call the Regulator?" he said, extending his hand.

"Been called that," Thompson said, taking the man's stubby fingers into his own.

"Good. Things sure'n hell need regulating up here. Took your time coming."

The range detective pulled off his narrow-brimmed hat, brushed at the sweat on his forehead with the palm of a hand. In a juniper nearby a half-dozen black-masked waxwings were feasting on the berries.

"Left same day I got your telegram," he said, stepping up onto the porch. "Was off doing a job so I don't know how long that sheriff'd been carrying it around."

"Was a month ago I sent it," McBride grumbled. "About to give up on you when I got your answer."

"Well, I'm here now," Thompson said dryly. "What kind of trouble you having?"

McBride stroked his handlebar moustache, gave the question a moment's thought. "Like I said in that there telegram, rustling, but that ain't all of it. Now, I've called the rest of the association in for a meeting tonight, right here at my place. I figure it best to let every man do his own talking, let you know what kind of problems he's got. There's not much sense in me hashing it all over now, but I reckon it won't hurt none to sort of give you the lay of the land."

Thompson, making no comment, crossed the porch and, squatting on his heels, put his back to the wall of the house. Taking a cigar from his case, he lit up, blew a cloud of smoke, and studied the rancher thoughtfully through the thin haze.

McBride, leaning against one of the round, wooden posts that supported the roof of the gallery, folded his arms across his chest. "You know where you are?"

Bill Thompson stirred indifferently. "New Mexico, maybe Colorado."

"Nope, you're across the line in what folks call the unorganized territory, or no-man's-land, or the Strip. Some even say the Panhandle. It's a piece of Oklahoma that none of the states or territories claim."

"Rode across it once," Thompson said. "Figured it'd been gobbled up in that land rush they had up here last spring."

"That was farther east. Panhandle was left alone . . . or maybe forgot. Anyway, that didn't have nothing to do with us. This here part of Oklahoma belongs to us — me and a dozen other ranchers — along with the worst collection of cutthroats and renegade outlaws that a man ever come across."

Thompson puffed slowly on his cigar. "These ranches all located in this no-man's-land?"

"Not all, and some that are lap over into Colorado or Kansas or New Mexico. There's even a couple that are partly in Texas, but mostly we're all in the Strip. Why?"

"Was wondering why the law —"

"Ain't none," McBride cut in flatly. "Nobody, not even a U.S. marshal or his deputies comes near us because they ain't got no authority up here. We don't pay no taxes to nobody — being a territory all on our own — and we look out for ourselves, settle our disputes without no help from anybody. Been doing it that way for years, but now things've got out of hand and it's come to where we figured best call in a professional. That's when we sent for you."

"Rustlers, mostly?"

"Mostly, but there's plenty of other devilment going on, too. Fact that there ain't no law leaves the Panhandle wide open for every outlaw there is that's on the dodge to hole up in. He can duck across the line into

43

our part of the country and there ain't no lawman can touch him.

"Makes it a roosting place for dozens of them, and they come and go as they please. Maybe they'll rob a stagecoach or a bank in some Kansas or Texas town, then beat it back here and hole up."

"They've got to spend their money some-where and Clayton's close by," Thompson observed. "Why don't the sheriff there or that eager-beaver U.S. deputy marshal —"

"Clevenger?"

"Yeh, Clevenger. Why don't they pick them up when they come into town?"

"Not where they head for. There's a place called Boston about twenty-five miles from here — in Colorado. Light out for it when they're flush."

"It a pretty good town?"

"Ain't nothing good about it — a bunch of saloons, cribs, a couple of stores. Started out to be a regular settlement for the home-steaders that moved in there thinking they'd found good farming country. All went busted because there wasn't no water — leastwise, not enough for growing crops. They pulled out and the outlaws took over. About all you'll find there nowadays."

"In Colorado — looks like they're lawmen could —"

"Well, they don't. Place just sets there like a big open sore, festering and rotting and causing trouble for all of us. What galls me most is they haul water from a spring on my land to keep the goddamn town going — not that they ever use much.

"Worst part of it is that all them painted women and saloons make it hard to keep hired hands on the job. Man thinks he's got a crew out working the range, finds out half of them are in Boston getting drunk and raising hell."

Thompson continued to puff at his cigar, his gaze reaching out across the rolling land to a dark smudge on the horizon . . . a herd of cattle on the move.

"Sounds like a right interesting place," he murmured after a while.

McBride groaned, swore feelingly. "Don't go telling me we'll have trouble with you hanging around there, swilling liquor. . . ."

"Nothing to worry about," the detective said with an offhand gesture. "Drinking ain't one of my shortcomings. And women — I can take them or leave them be. I was thinking: if it's such a real popular place with the hardcase bunch, just who all a man might meet was he to walk down the street."

A look of relief spread across John

McBride's face. "Sure glad to hear you say that, but there won't be no reason for your going there — leastwise none that I can see. You'll be working inside the Panhandle and maybe getting across the line now and then. Like I've said, me and the other ranchers make up the government here and we furnish our own law, but it's only good inside our borders."

Thompson removed the cigar from his mouth. "That mean I've got to pull up if I'm tracking some jasper and he rides over into Kansas or one of the other states?"

"Going to leave that up to you. Be your judgment."

The range detective relaxed, clenched the cigar between his teeth again. Two riders swung into the yard, stared curiously at him and McBride, and proceeded on to the hitchrack at the end of the bunkhouse. Over in the kitchen the cook was banging pots and pans around as he began to prepare the evening meal.

"But that's something we'd best hold off getting into until the rest of the association gets here," the rancher continued. "Soon's I heard you'd hit town, I sent word for them to come."

"Been wondering about that. How'd you know I'd got here?"

McBride smiled. "One of my hands was in Clayton when you had your little palaver with Noah Clevenger. He brung the word to me. Was here quite a time before you, so I reckon you must've took it easy."

Thompson nodded. "Had myself a look-see at the country."

"All you've seen was the New Mexico side of it, though I reckon the rest ain't much different. More hay growing east and north of here makes it some prettier, but a rock's a rock, and a wash is a wash."

"For sure," Bill murmured. "What time's the meeting to be?"

"Seven o'clock. Take some of the men that long to get here. We're strung out all along the line — the Strip's a good hundred and thirty miles long and maybe forty wide. Most of them won't have to ride that far, of course, but that'll give you a rough idea of how much territory you'll be looking after."

"Going to be a fair-sized chore."

"Can bet on it, but you'll get your price, whatever it'll be, if you do the job — and we aim to give you some help."

Again Thompson paused, removed the cigar from his clenched teeth. "Help? What kind?"

"Deputies. We got a couple lined up."

The man known as the Regulator wagged

his head disapprovingly. "Can forget that. I work alone."

McBride frowned, rubbed at his jaw. "Best you think that over."

"Why? Way I've been doing for years."

"Maybe so, but up here it's going to be a mite different. Word gets out you're working for us, there'll be a dozen gunslingers looking to pot you in the back. You'll need them deputies to watch your hindside, but we can hash that over later, too.

"Now, it's getting on to suppertime. I want you to eat with me and my missus here in the house. Turn your horse over to the hostler down at the barn and let him take care of him — he'll do whatever you tell him. Then you can wash up if you're of a mind at the pump out behind the bunkhouse that the rest of the boys use.

"When you're done, come on back up here. Grub'll be ready by then, and time we're done eating the association members'll be showing up. Can settle any questions you've got on your mind then — if you've got any."

"There's a couple," Thompson said blandly, and drawing himself erect, crossed to the buckskin, mounted, and rode across the hard-packed yard to the barn.

5

Bill Thompson and John McBride had finished the evening meal and were taking their ease in two of the several chairs the rancher had brought out and placed on the porch when the first of the association members arrived.

It was shortly after sundown and a deep amber glow lay upon the land lending it a soft-edged calmness. Birds called softly from the trees clustered about the spring that served the ranchhouse, and high in the rose-streaked sky to the west ducks were winging southward.

"This here'll be Amos Lindeman," McBride said as a rancher, alone on the seat of well-used buckboard, wheeled into the yard and halted.

Thompson, eyes on the man, nodded. "Where's his place?"

"South of me — about ten mile."

Lindeman, blond, squat, wearing a hat with an unusually wide brim that made it look much too large for him, climbed down from the vehicle with painful slowness and started for the porch. He walked with a decided limp.

"Amos ain't as old as you might figure," McBride said in a low voice. "Maybe forty-five or so, but he's all stove-up. Got stomped by a horse a few years back, left him crippled up some."

Lindeman reached the edge of the porch, halted, bobbed to McBride, and extended his hand to Thompson.

"Reckon you're that range detective we've been waiting for."

Bill nodded, returned the greeting, and settled back again into his chair as Lindeman selected one of the leather rockers and made himself comfortable. Almost at once two riders entered the yard at a lope, veered into the rack.

"Charlie Gere and Clete Potter," McBride said as the pair dismounted. "Leaves only Henry —"

"He'll be late," Lindeman muttered. "Always is."

Gere was considerably younger than the others, Thompson noted, being somewhere in his early thirties. Husky, redheaded, with pale-blue eyes, he had a youthful urgency about him that seemed to chafe the others. Clete Potter, on the other hand, was a lean, drawling Texan who sank smilingly into his chair after the introductions were over and lapsed into a silence, evidently content to let his fellow association members engineer the proceedings.

Talk was desultory, ran mostly to the current condition of the range: dry with the promise of an early winter; beef prices: not as good as they should be probably because there were getting to be too damned many outfits supplying the market; and various family matters.

Thompson listened idly, eyes half closed, hearing only scraps of what was being said. The ranchers were carefully avoiding any conversation concerning the reason for his being there, evidently holding off until the last of the association could put in an appearances — a man they called Henry who customarily was tardy at meetings. He would bring the membership total to five — not a very large organization for so vast a country, Bill decided, giving it thought.

The latecomer, Henry Davidson, arrived shortly before full dark, a tall, lank man in a business suit and driving a fairly new buggy. He made his apologies, shook hands with Bill soberly, and dropped into one of the remaining chairs.

"Expect we're ready to begin," he said.

Thompson, impelled more by curiosity than by any other reason, said, "This all there is to your association — five members?"

"There's more," Davidson replied. "It's just that they sort of leave things up to us — we being the ones with the biggest ranches and having the most at stake." He paused, glanced at McBride. "What about Court and Lacey?"

"They'll be coming along later. Frank had some getting ready to do and Jim's waiting for him."

Davidson put his attention back on Thompson. "They're the deputies we're furnishing."

The detective stirred, listened momentarily to the far-off yelping of a coyote greeting the night. "McBride told me. I don't need any help — always work alone."

Davidson brushed at his mouth, glanced about questioningly, frowned. "Reckon you'd best reconsider that, Thompson. You'll need Jim Court and Frank Lacey. Between them they know this country inside and out, which'll save you a hell of a lot of useless riding, and they'll be there to watch your back while you're doing it."

The range detective grinned faintly.

"Folks're sure worried about my backside, it seems. Never had no trouble before."

"Doubt if you've ever worked a country where there's more renegades and back-shooters per square mile running loose than there is up here," Amos Lindeman said dryly.

Thompson shrugged. It seemed he was to have a couple of deputies whether he wanted them or not. So be it; he'd rid himself of them later if he found it necessary.

McBride motioned to Davidson. "I ain't told him much, Henry. You best run over the whole thing."

Davidson drew a blackened pipe from his coat pocket, cupped it in the palm of a hand. "Rustlers, horse thieves, squatters by the dozen — that's what our trouble is," he said, now taking a pouch of tobacco from a different pocket and tamping a quantity of the shredded weed into the charred bowl. "Was a time when we could take care of it ourselves, but the country's gone plumb loco since they opened up Oklahoma and we just can't handle it no more."

"Squatters are really getting bad," Charlie Gere added. "Any man that takes the notion can move onto the Panhandle, throw up some kind of a shack, and start home-steading. There ain't no law that says he can't, and there ain't none that says he can. It's all open, free land, and they figure they got the right."

"Which I reckon they have," McBride said, "but this ain't farming country and usually it ain't farming they aim to do. They're nothing but trash, spongers. They just squat there and live on our beef, stealing them one, maybe two at a time. Was they serious about homesteading I reckon none of us would give a damn, but they ain't."

"We was here first," Gere declared. "Gives us prior range rights — right of possession I hear it's called — and, by God, I —"

"I'm not going to argue about it," Thompson cut in mildly as the young rancher's voice rose to a peak of indignation. "Main thing I want to know is if I've got a free hand to stop it."

Davidson, holding a match to his pipe, paused, said, "Meaning?"

"Just this. A rustler's a rustler whether he steals one steer or fifty. Same goes for a horse thief. They all look alike to me and I handle them the same way — my way. If any of you've got a soft spot, now's the time to speak up, let me know. I don't work for bleeding hearts."

Again Davidson looked about at his fellow members. "Well, we sure want it all stopped — the rustling and the nesting and such," he said finally, "but you'll be working for us and we feel we ought to have some say-so."

Thompson came forward in his chair, removed the lifeless cigar butt from between his teeth. "Maybe you've picked the wrong man," he said bluntly. "Never was much of a hand to work with strings tied to me."

"He's right," Clete Potter said, coming into the discussion for the first time. "We hire him to get the job done — letting him do it his way makes sense."

McBride and Gere voiced their approval. Davidson glanced questioningly at Lindeman, who nodded.

"All right, you do what you have to do," the rancher said, giving in, "but it's best you remember this: your authority, and we intend to swear you in as our marshal, only covers the Panhandle."

Thompson nodded. "I understand. It make any difference where I set up my headquarters?"

"All done for you. McBride's fixed up one of his line shacks up in the northwest corner of his range just for that. You and Lacey and Jim Court'll be bunking there. We'll keep you supplied with grub and water and spare horses."

"Can do your patrolling from there real easy," McBride said, "besides putting you where we can get word to you quick when something turns up."

"We don't want any more squatters moving in," Gere added. "Got enough of them hanging around now that we'd like to be rid of. Anyways, most of them roosting on the range now ain't nothing but hard-cases dodging the law and looking to lay low till things cool off for them. Meantime they're stealing cows, eating off us —"

"You want them moved off?"

"You're goddamn right we do — and we don't want a fresh batch sneaking in after they're gone, either!"

"They ain't all outlaws," Lindeman began, shaking his head. "I figure we ought use a little common sense."

"We've already told Thompson we'd leave it up to him," Potter reminded the rancher.

McBride started to speak, fell silent, and half turned around in his chair, his attention on the gate. Darkness was almost complete and the two riders swinging up to the hitchrack were no more than indistinct blurs.

"Here's Lacey and Jim Court now," he said. "Was beginning to think they weren't going to make it."

The riders halted, dismounted, strode

briskly to the porch. Thompson, not rising from his chair and clearly indifferent, acknowledged the introductions with no more than a nod of his head. Court, a young man in his early twenties, was a slender, intense individual who evidently was taking his appointment as a deputy with deep seriousness. Frank Lacey was considerably older, in his forties probably, and was a settled, cool sort of man.

When they had backed off and found places to sit on the edge of the porch, Davidson took a few minutes to review the particulars that had been covered, and then advised them that, under Bill Thompson's supervision, they were ready to go to work.

"As president of the Cattleman's Association, I am officially appointing Thompson here as marshal of the Neutral Territory and you two as his deputies, with full authority to apprehend and bring in lawbreakers."

"Who'll we be turning prisoners over to?" Lacey asked when Davidson had finished.

"Probably Noah Clevenger in Clayton'll be the best bet — and he's the closest."

Thompson leaned forward, took the cigar butt from his mouth again, and started to speak. He hesitated as the door of the house opened and McBride's wife, followed by their cook, came out onto the porch. The woman was carrying a lamp, the man had a coffeepot and a number of the tin cups on a tray.

Silent, the men half rose in polite deference to McBride's wife, settled back again, and watched her place the lamp in a bracket on the wall and move aside while the cook distributed the cups and filled them with steaming, black liquid. Still without speaking, both turned and reentered the house when the ritual-like proceedings were finished.

"Was right nice of Martha," Davidson said then, nodding to McBride. "Appreciate your telling her so for me, for all of us."

"Sure will," McBride replied, and shifted his gaze to Thompson. "Was there something you was about to say, Marshal?"

Bill thought for a moment. He had intended to remind the ranchers of their promise of no interference, having his doubts, from previous experience, as to the number of prisoners they could expect to hand over to U.S. Deputy Marshal Noah Clevenger, but reckoned there was no need. He'd simply get to work, go about his business, and let matters take their course.

"Nope, guess not," he said, and took a deep swallow of the coffee. Turning his eyes to his two assistants, he continued. "We moving into that line shack tonight?"

"Might as well," Lacey said. "We're all set."

"If you're of a mind," McBride suggested before the detective could answer, "you can stay the night here in my bunkhouse."

Thompson drained his cup, put it aside, and rose. "Just as soon get settled," he said, and crossing the porch, stepped down into the yard. "I'll get my horse," he finished, nodding to the deputies, and moved off into the darkness.

McBride and his brother ranchers watched Bill Thompson, flanked by Lacey and Court, ride across the yard and disappear into the night.

"Sure is a odd one," Amos Lindeman said in a doubtful voice. "I'm wondering if we've made the right move."

"Far as I'm concerned, we have," Gere stated in a flat, positive way. "Way I see it he's exactly what we've been needing. Government won't give us no help, so we got no choice but to get our own — and hiring on the best there is, is smart."

"I reckon he's the best — or the worst, all depending on how you look at it," Lindeman murmured.

"Wondering a bit about him myself," Henry Davidson said then, starting to refill his pipe for the drive home. "Going to be a right smart of a job keeping him pointed the direction we want."

"We'll be wise not to even try," Clete Potter drawled. "Leave the man be. He knows what we want done and how best to do it."

Davidson stepped down off the porch. "Yeh, reckon that's right. We hired him and we'd be fools to be sorry before he even starts working."

"I ain't about to be sorry!" Charlie Gere declared, also moving off the gallery. "I've lost all the beef I aim to, and if it takes a bounty hunter —"

"Range detective," McBride corrected sharply.

"All right, a range detective that believes in shooting first and asking questions later, then I'm all for him."

"Amen to that," Clete Potter said, and headed for his horse.

6

The ride across the starlit prairie, glowing like old silver in the pale night, to the not too distant line shack where a base would be maintained by Thompson and his deputies was made with few words being spoken and those only of necessity.

Once there and the horses secured in the wagon-shedlike shelter provided for them off one end of the shack, the men moved up to the entrance.

"Lantern's hanging there near the door," Frank Lacey said, stepping past the detective. "I'll light it."

Bill halted, allowed the man to take down the Dietz. Tripping the lever and striking a match on the seat of his trousers, the deputy held it to the wick until a wedge of flame sprang into life. Resetting the globe, he pushed open the door and led the way into the room.

There were four bunks built against two of the walls, and Thompson, showing no particular preference, crossed to the nearest, dropped his saddlebags and blanket roll upon it. Wheeling then, he let his small eyes sweep the remainder of the room — complete with a small cook stove, utensils, chairs, a table, and a stock of groceries neatly arranged on a stack of shelves. Lacey and Jim Court watched him intently, the latter almost with anxiety.

"It ain't much —" the young man said.

"Line shacks never are," Thompson replied. "Makes no difference. Don't expect to be around much."

"Frank here's a pretty good cook," Court continued. "We sure ain't going to go hungry."

"No problem," the detective said, shrugging, and raked the pair with his abrasive glance. "Like to get something straight. Usually I work alone. Didn't expect the association to saddle me with a couple of helpers, but they seem to want it that way. All right, that's how we'll do it. All I'll ask of you is that you keep out from under foot and look out for yourself."

Lacey nodded, grinned wryly. "Sort of got the idea of how you felt back there at McBride's."

"Nothing personal —"

"We know that, but the ranchers all felt you'd need some help. I don't think you realize how bad things are up here — outlaws, killers all of them, running loose all over the place. Word spreads that you've taken the job to clean them out, there'll be a half-dozen looking for a chance to put a bullet in you."

Thompson's thick shoulders stirred. "I've got a knack for staying alive. It's got me by this long, expect it'll keep on doing it."

Lacey said, "Up to you, of course, but if it's all the same, we'll tag along." He paused, glanced at his young partner. "Truth is, the pay's good and we need the job."

Thompson's mouth split into a humorless smile. "Don't try to slick-talk me, friend," he said, sitting down on the edge of his bunk. "That's been tried by experts and I don't buy. You both been working steady. Now, just keep out of my way and we'll get along fine."

Pushing his saddlebags off onto the floor, Bill placed his blanket roll at the head of the bunk for a pillow and, still fully dressed, stretched out and fell asleep immediately.

Thompson was up early that next morning, and with Lacey and Court still snoring in their bunks, he crossed to the stove, built a fire, and set a pot of water to heating for coffee. Before he had finished the chore, the deputies had aroused and Lacey, hurriedly pulling on his clothing, stepped in.

"I'll take over," he offered.

Thompson did not look around. "Coffee's all I'm after."

The deputy reached for a large glass jar on one of the shelves that contained already crushed beans. "Have it for you in a couple of minutes. Pancakes suit you for breakfast?"

"Just coffee."

Lacey tipped back the lid of the pot, poured a generous amount of dark-brown grains into the now-simmering water. "Man's got to eat."

"Now and then," Thompson agreed with no show of interest.

"You ain't figuring on regular meals?" Jim Court asked. He was still on the edge of his bunk, drawing on his boots.

"Out of the regular habit. Eat when I get the feeling."

Lacey pushed the coffee to one side of the stove where it could cool and the grounds settle. "Best way then for me to handle that, I expect, is to cook up a big pot of beans and salt pork, along with a mess of biscuits and have them handy. Can help yourself anytime you take the notion."

"That'll suit me fine," Thompson said, picking up one of the tin cups. "You reckon that java's ready?"

Lacey, using a fold of rag as a hot pad, took up the pot. "Ain't settled good yet," he said, and filled the cup.

Thompson made no comment and, drink in hand, turned to the door. Opening it, he stepped out into the early-morning light. Lacey was like an old hen, he thought, determined to look out for him, and young Jim Court, probably hopeful of becoming a lawman someday, was going to be one who got underfoot. He'd best figure to sidetrack them when he got started to work; an eager pair like them could get a man killed.

"Sure you don't want to stock up on some pancakes?" Lacey called from inside the cabin.

Thompson, eyes drifting aimlessly across the timothy-clad slopes of the low hills, tipped his cup of black coffee to his lips and finished it off.

"Nope," he answered, and paused as a rider broke into view on the crest of a rise to the east. He watched the distant figure grow steadily more distinct as it approached for a time, and then stepping back into the line shack, he helped himself to a second cup of the coffee.

"Somebody's coming," Jim Court announced suddenly. "Running his horse pretty hard from the sound of it."

At once Lacey and the younger man hurried to the door and glanced out. Thompson, cup in hand, pivoted slowly, took up a stand behind them.

"It's Ike Pickett," Court said, squinting into the now-breaking sunlight.

"One of Amos Lindeman's hired hands," Lacey explained over his shoulder to the detective. "Must be some trouble — dammit, my pancakes!" he added, breaking off abruptly and wheeling hurriedly back to the stove.

Thompson regarded the man with a half smile, pushed by Court, and stepped out onto the hardpack fronting the shack. Pickett was now only a hundred yards or so away and coming on fast.

"Where's Lacey?" the cowhand shouted as he drew up at the rack. "There's been some rustling —"

"Never mind Lacey," Thompson cut in gruffly. "What about some rustling?"

Pickett, a young man about the same age as Jim Court, swallowed hard. He shifted his glance briefly to the doorway of the cabin, then back to Thompson.

"Lindeman sent me. Was two rustlers seen driving off about ten, maybe twelve head of stock last night. Lindeman wants you all to go after them, bring them in."

Thompson pivoted, reentered the shack, and dropped his empty cup onto the table. Lacey, cooking chore done with, had a plate stacked high with thick pancakes and was setting them on the back of the stove where they could keep warm.

"You say somebody seen the rustlers?" he said to Pickett as the rider came into the cabin. "Where?"

"Was headed toward Tolan's Wash?"

"Where's that from here?" Thompson asked, moving to the door.

"Hard to tell you," Lacey said, and turning to his bunk, took up his hat and belted gun. "Save time to just take you there."

Thompson had not slowed his step. He shook his head. "I reckon I could find it."

"Yeh, expect you could, but it might be too late time you did. If you aim to nail them red-handed, you'd best let Jim and me lead the way."

The range detective nodded. "All right, but let's get moving."

7

They rode south and west from the line shack, Lacey and Court flanking the silent Bill Thompson. After a time the wide, almost level flat across which they were moving began to break up into small gullies, finally sloped down into a broad, deep, brush-filled arroyo.

"Tolan's Wash is over that way," Lacey said, pointing to a ragged bluff a mile or so farther on. "That's the south wall. There's an old two-story rock house up at the head of it."

"Nobody lives there?"

"Not regular like. Place has been standing empty for years excepting for the drifters that hole up there now and then."

"I expect that's where we'll find those rustlers."

"More'n likely," Lacey agreed. "Were seen heading that direction, and it wouldn't be the first time it's been used as a cow camp where some brand changing could be done."

Thompson raked the buckskin with his spurs, increased the pace to a steady lope, and with the deputies at his side, pointed directly for the wash. A short distance above he raised a hand, slowed the party to a walk, wanting to take no chances on the outlaws hearing the hoofbeats of the horses.

"Wait here," he said, motioning for the two men to halt. "I'll have a look."

Lacey shook his head. "Best we all go along, Marshal. Hard to figure what you'll be running into. Could be more'n two rustlers in the bunch — if that's where they are."

Thompson started to voice an objection, let it slide as his eyes picked up a thin spiral of smoke beginning to rise from the lower end of the wash. A branding fire, he concluded, and kept the buckskin moving at a fast walk.

Lacey and Court had spotted the smoke. The older man said, "There's a bit of a bluff at the lower end of the wash. Can easy see what's going on below from its rim."

"Lead the way," the detective said.

Lacey immediately swung off, began to curve toward the foot of the deep slash where it opened up into the arroyo. Reaching a mound of rocks and weed, he pulled to a halt.

"Best we walk from here."

Thompson dismounted, hitched at his pistol, and started for the crest rising before him. The smoke streamer, a short distance to their right now, had thickened, and once they heard the clang of metal striking some hard surface.

Gaining the top of the bluff, Thompson dropped flat and, with Lacey and Court following suit, crawled to the edge of the formation and threw his attention down into the deep cut. Jim Court, at his left shoulder, swore softly.

There were two men. Both were hunched beside a low fire into which a branding iron had been thrust to heat. Nearby, in a hastily built corral of rope and brush, were nine steers.

"Got them red-handed," Lacey murmured.

"Those Lindeman's steers?" Thompson asked, wanting to make certain.

"Spade's brand's on them," Court said. "They're Lindeman's."

The range detective pulled back, got to his feet. "I'm going down. You two wait here with the horses."

Lacey, also drawing away from the rim so as not to become silhouetted, frowned. "I figure we'd all best go —"

"You wait here," Thompson repeated in a flat, unyielding way. "I'll sing out when I need you and my horse."

He moved off at once, cutting down around the end of the bluff and turning into the wash from the arroyo. Walking quietly for so heavy a man, he approached the rustlers. A dozen yards or so short of the two hunched figures a startled rabbit shot out from under his feet, raced off into the brush. Instantly the outlaws sprang erect.

"Hold — right where you are!" Thompson shouted.

For answer the pair ducked back into the thick brush. Thompson charged forward, drew to a stop as the quick thud of hooves sounded. The rustlers were fleeing up the wash.

Bill shifted his attention to the rim of the bluff overhead. Lacey and Court were looking down at him. He beckoned impatiently.

"Bring the horses."

Both men disappeared at once, reappeared shortly at the foot of the wash. Thompson, arms folded and unmoving, waited until they drew abreast and then swung up onto his saddle.

"Can they get out of this canyon at the upper end?"

71

"Not on horses," Lacey said. "Probably aim to hole up in the old house."

Thompson roweled the buckskin, started him up the grade. There had once been a fairly wide road winding a course between the rocks and cedar trees, but now thickly growing brush and boulders, loosened by rainstorms and rolling down from the higher levels of the slopes, combined to all but obliterate it.

Abruptly the stone house came into view. The rustlers had abandoned their horses and, as Lacey had prophesied, had taken refuge within the thick-walled structure. Dismounting again, the range detective walked ahead to where he could have an unimpeded look at the old building.

"You — inside the house!" he called. "Come out with your hands over your head!"

"Go to hell!" a muffled voice answered.

Immediately gunshots crackled from the lower floor of the structure. Dust spurted around Thompson's booted feet, and jerking to one side, he dropped to a crouch behind a low shoulder of rocks, began to return the outlaw's fire. From behind another mound off to his left Court and Frank Lacey also opened up.

For a full half hour shots were exchanged,

and then Thompson, motioning to the deputies to hold off and keeping well out of sight, called to the rustlers again.

"Giving you your last chance. Throw your guns down and come out. You ain't getting out of there alive."

"And you ain't getting in alive, either!" one of the outlaws declared, and snapped two quick shots in the direction of the detective.

Bill shrugged and, dropping back, circled to where the deputies had taken their stand. Removing his hat, he brushed at the sweat on his forehead and glanced up the wash to the old house.

"Got us a Mexican standoff," he said. "Going to need some dynamite — about a half-dozen sticks and the stuff to set them off with."

Lacey stared. "You figure to blow up the place?"

Thompson considered the deputy coldly. "You think of a better way to get them out?"

Lacey wagged his head. Jim Court said, "Sounds like a good idea to me."

"Then get me some dynamite."

"There'll be some at that spring just below the butte," the young deputy said. "McBride keep a box handy for cleaning it out, always filling up with dirt."

"How long'll it take you to get there and back?"

"Hour, maybe."

Thompson nodded. "Make it fast. It's going to get hot waiting here," he said, leaning up against the weedy mound.

Court, ducking low, pivoted and returned to where they had left the horses. As he mounted up, Bill came partly about, fired a bullet at the house.

"Got to keep them pinned down. Keep shooting," he said, and pulled back.

Lacey, taking the opportunity to reload his weapon, exchanged shots with the outlaws, and then, taking his cue from Thompson, settled down. The range detective, slumped against a rock, hat tipped forward over his eyes, appeared to be dozing, but it was far from that. Every few minutes he would rise, throw a shot or two at the house, aiming always for the empty, gaping windows from which the rustlers were doing their shooting; after that, he would again relax.

Uncommunicative, he gave only monosyllabic replies to the questions and comments Frank Lacey made in an effort to start a conversation, and when Jim Court returned slightly more than an hour after riding out, hardly two dozen words had been traded by the two men.

Taking the explosive, Thompson got to his feet, spent a few moments having a thorough look at the house and its surrounding area while be considered the problem. He'd be exposed to the outlaws for the first dozen or so yards, he saw, but beyond that the rocks and brush on the north slope of the wash would afford ample protection. Drawing his pistol, he started to move out.

"You going up there with that dynamite?" Lacey asked in an awed tone.

"What the hell you think I got it for?" Thompson answered without pausing.

"Figured you were going to throw it."

"A stick at a time won't do any good — not against those rock walls. Got to plant it."

"You're putting yourself in the open," the deputy persisted. "We best give you some covering fire."

"Up to you," the detective said, and darting from behind the mound, shooting as he ran, legged it for the nearest of the rocks that offered protection.

Bullets whipped about him: some thudded into the dry soil; others, screeching away into space as they struck solid surface, glanced off. He heard Lacey and Jim Court open up and for a brief moment the shooting from the house ceased, and then he was behind the first of the big rocks and safe from the rustlers' reach.

Pausing long enough to get his breath, Bill again had a probing look at the house and close-by area. He'd do best by circling, come in from the rear, upper corner of the structure. Such would permit him to slip in, place the dynamite where it would be the most effective.

Continuing, Thompson worked his way across the north side of the wash, only vaguely aware that the two deputies were maintaining a steady exchange with the outlaws. Coming to a point where he could drop down off the grade and reach the old house, he halted once more, made ready the dynamite sticks thoughtfully arranged by John McBride or one of his ranch hands into a tight bundle, and resumed the descent.

Drawing near the structure, Thompson spotted a break in its rock foundation, and crawling the remainder of the distance, he carefully set the explosive in the opening, pushing it in under the house as far as possible. Stringing the somewhat short fuse out to its full length, he struck a match to its end and hurried back across the slope.

He was little more than halfway to where Lacey and Court were waiting when the dynamite went off. There was a deafening roar, a rushing wall of air, and a great surging cloud of dust filled with bits of rock and wood lifted upward, hung briefly, and then settled back into the wash as echoes rolled to all directions.

Thompson, calmly dusting himself, turned, walked slowly into the center of the now-smoking rubble, eyes searching for the two outlaws. Moments later he located their bodies and, avoiding several small fires, crossed to them. Brushing aside bits of litter, he gave the face of each a close look and then came fully around.

"That's sure the end of them two."

The voice of young Jim Court brought him to a stop. The deputy's eyes were bright with excitement. From beyond him Lacey spoke.

"They didn't have no chance, not against that dynamite."

The range detective's jaw hardened. "You're wrong," he said coldly. "They could've quit. I made the offer twice."

Frank Lacey, eyes fixed on the still-drifting layers of dust and smoke, shook his head slowly. "Yeh, you did, but using dynamite . . ."

Thompson swore quietly. "It make a difference to you how they died? Would it've been better if I'd just shot them down?"

"Seems more fitting."

"You're a fool, Lacey!" the detective snapped. "In this business you use whatever you can to get the job done. You go being nice and polite about how you finish off an outlaw and it'll be you that winds up dead. Come on, let's get them steers and head them back to Lindeman's. Sun's getting hot."

He took a step, hauled up short again. Amos Lindeman, with John McBride, was hurrying toward him. Their weathered features were taut, filled with concern. Thompson sighed deeply, folded his arms across his ample front, and settled back on his heels. Both ranchers were looking past him at the wreckage of the old house.

"You blowed the place to hell!" Lindeman said in a strained voice. "Was them rustlers —"

Bill Thompson nodded. "Were holed up inside. Couldn't get them out."

McBride mopped at his face with a bandanna.

"Would've liked for you to bring them in so's we could hang them, legal. That way they'd served as a warning to others."

Thompson shrugged. "From what you told me about conditions up here, I figure it's too late for warnings. Thing to do is act."

"But killing them with dynamite —"

"They had their chance to give up," Jim Court said, moving up beside Thompson. "Twice the marshal told them to throw down their guns, but they same as told him to go to hell and kept right on shooting. He done what he had to."

Bill half turned, regarded the young deputy, a faint smile of approval on his lips. Maybe there was some hope for the boy after all. He came back to the ranchers.

"I'll be reminding you both of our deal — no bleeding hearts. I do my job, my way."

"Sure, sure," McBride said hastily. "We ain't going to interfere. Just sort of set us back on our haunches when we heard that blast and realized what was going on."

Lindeman slapped his big hands together. "Well, it sure fixed them — the place, too. Won't be no renegades hanging out here in Tolan's Wash from now on. I reckon we ought to thank the marshal for that."

"Guess you're right," McBride said. "Now, if the same thing'd happen to that hell-hole, Boston, we'd be shut of another big problem."

"Want to thank you, too, for getting me back my stock," Lindeman continued. "First time in many a year. I'm sure obliged."

Thompson drew out his metal case, selected a cigar, and thrust it between his teeth. "What you're paying me for," he said, and started on down the trail.

8

Boston . . .

Thompson, hunched in the midmorning shade alongside the line shack that next day, let his thoughts settle on the outlaw town. He was recalling not only the things he'd been told about the place but also John McBride's offhand remark to the effect that its destruction, like that visited upon the old house in Tolan's Wash, would be welcome.

He was alone. Jim Court had gone to Davidson's Bar-Cross Ranch on a personal errand of some sort, and Frank Lacey had been delegated to pack the bodies of the two rustlers into Clayton for burial, where a report of their deaths could be made to the authorities.

It had been Bill's plan to make a wide, patrolling sweep of the range, beginning that morning, but the absence of the deputies had dictated he remain at the shack where he could be reached should something develop that required his immediate services.

He'd like to have a look at Boston and the

crowd that hung around it. He just might run into somebody he'd long been searching for, it being a haven for any and every outlaw that honed to keep out of sight. It was beyond his "jurisdiction," of course. That had been made plain to him — but hell, he didn't intend going there as the marshal of the Panhandle, but only as a visitor.

The detective mulled the matter over thoroughly. There was no real need for him to just sit around the line shack. He could leave a note for Jim Court, who would be returning shortly; the deputy could watch the store, and if anything important arose where he was needed, Jim could come after him. Boston was only a short ride away.

Coming to a decision, Bill Thompson came to his feet, entered the shack. Scribbling the necessary message to the young deputy, he placed it on the table where it could not be overlooked, and then, saddling his buckskin, he rode out.

He reached the settlement around midday, halted at the side of a sagging, deserted building that stood at the extreme end of the town's one street, to have his look. Boston wasn't much, as he'd been told; two or three saloons, a general store with windows glazed by dust, a livery stable, several abandoned structures, and a fairly large house, set apart, that probably had once been the residence of the town's most important family.

There was no one abroad, but horses were standing at the hitchracks of the saloons and in the corral at the stable. As Bill watched, a cowhand, still wearing his chaps as if he had just ridden in off the range, came from one of the saloons. A woman clad in a bright-yellow, but ragged and soiled dress clung to his arm. They moved immediately if unsteadily toward the large house, which now apparently served as a base of operations for the woman and others of her profession.

Raking the buckskin with his spurs, Thompson rode on into the settlement, swinging past the neglected buildings until he reached another vacant structure at the opposite end of town. There, dismounting, he picketed the gelding in the shadows behind the old building where he would not be seen, and dropping back to the street, headed for the first of the saloons in line.

There was no door to the place, and when he stepped into the shadowy room, no particular notice was taken of his arrival by the half-dozen or so patrons slouching at the crude bar. Halting at the counter, he nodded to the man behind it and pointed at a bottle from which others were being served.

"Whiskey."

The bartender took a glass from a bucket of water, shook the excess drops from it, and filled it to the brim.

"Two bits," he said, setting it on the rough surface of the counter.

Thompson dropped a quarter beside the glass, wheeled, hooked his elbows on the edge of the bar, and glanced around. He saw no familiar faces. A woman sitting at a table in a back corner pulled herself upright wearily, considered him with tired eyes. He shook his head and she settled again into her chair. The place was dead — and there was no one of interest to him present.

Turning, he took up his drink, downed it, and cutting across the room, gained the door and stepped again into the open. Walking slowly through the loose dust, thick shoulders slumped, eyes taking in everything of note along the way, he continued until he reached the next saloon. Immediately he was aware of a low, steady rumble of noise.

He'd been in the wrong place, Thompson realized as he pushed through a pair of scarred, batwing doors into what a faded sign proclaimed the Palace. The saloon, a large square area lighted by several circular chandeliers, was crowded with customers, some strung out along a bar that stood against a back wall, others taking their ease at tables or clustered in a section of the room where gambling was underway. A dozen or more women were in evidence and an elderly, bearded piano player sat on a chair at his instrument enjoying an interlude while the nearby square of floor reserved for dancing was deserted.

Thompson paused just within the entrance to light a cigar and allow his eyes to completely adjust to the change. When his vision had cleared fully, he swept the room with a probing glance, felt a stir as he recognized several men — outlaws all — that he had encountered in the past and had cause to remember.

Suddenly cool and wary, he started across to the bar, conscious of the attention his presence was drawing, of the distinct lull in conversations. But if such disturbed him, it did not show in the easy, indifferent manner in which he moved.

Reaching the end of the counter, he halted, raised his small, deep-set eyes, and returned the stares of the men ranged along its length. At his level gaze they all, as one, looked away, and slowly the undercurrent of sound began to resume.

"Bill, by God —"

The detective shifted his attention to the bartender, who had stepped up to serve him. He nodded to the man — Jace Connors, a onetime stagecoach driver from over in Texas.

"Howdy, Jace," he said, his voice, as always, betraying no emotion. "Never expected to find you around here."

"Goes for me, too, Bill," the barman replied, frowning. "You looking to get yourself killed?"

"Not if I can help it."

"Well, you sure as hell are asking for it! Place is crawling with jaspers that'd like nothing more'n to square up with you for something you done to them or some of their kin."

"Big reason I rode by — was sort of anxious to see who was around. Heard the town was a hideout for half the outlaws in the country. Who's the bull of the woods?"

"Red King," Connors said, taking up a glass and pouring Thompson a drink. "Him and his whole bunch — Art Lea, Durham, Ed Cherry, Dutch Reiker, and some others you maybe don't know."

"Possible," the detective said. "Ain't many of them I've missed."

Jace Connors glanced about the room. "Red ain't here now. Neither's Lea and a couple of the others, but Dutch and Cherry're setting over there in the corner. You come here looking for Red?"

"Nope. Like I said, I just dropped by. I'm working for some ranchers over in the Panhandle — the neutral territory. Cleaning out rustlers for them. Was told about this town, got to wondering who I'd find here."

"Just about anybody the law'd like to lay hands on."

"That include you?"

Connors shrugged. "Maybe, but it ain't nothing you'd be interested in."

"Glad to hear that," Thompson said, and tossed off his drink. "You say Red's not around?"

"Rode over Texas way — him and a half-dozen others."

"Going after a bank or something, I expect."

"Who knows? I make it a point to mind my own business. It ain't healthy, otherwise."

"You own this place?"

"No, Red does — leastwise, I guess you can say he does. Town's his and Art Lea's —

they've got the most gunnies and that makes them the boss. Why? You aiming to take on Red?"

"Not especially unless he starts rustling cattle and stealing horses over in my bailiwick."

Connors gave that thought, finally nodded. "He ain't apt to fool with none of that. Small time for him nowadays, but he ain't going to like it when he hears you've been here."

"Sure can't help that none," Thompson murmured.

A scuffle broke out in the back of the area where the gamblers were holding forth. Connors moved off a step for a better look. The bartender at the opposite end of the counter started to forsake his post and investigate the disturbance, changed his mind when the commotion abruptly ceased. Jace Connors eased back to where he had been standing. His features were stiff, sober.

"You been spotted, Bill," he said, making a show of wiping up the counter. "Seen Ed Cherry looking this way, then he said something to Dutch, and he started looking. You done me a big favor once and I feel I owe you, so when you get ready to leave, I'll slip you out the back door."

"No need," Thompson said. "And far as

you owing me — that's been forgot a long time ago. I don't bring balances forward like some bookkeeper."

Connors rubbed nervously at his jaw with his free hand. Then, laying the towel aside, he refilled the range detective's glass.

"They're still looking. Kind of eyeing me, too, like they figure I'm maybe a mite too friendly. Hope you won't mind if I keep this sort of businesslike."

"You do what you want," Thompson said, and reaching into a pocket produced half a dollar and laid it on the counter. "That enough?"

"Enough," Connors said. "Mind telling me what you aim to do?"

"Walk out of here," Thompson said flatly. "Got my horse standing at the edge of town. I'm going to get on him and ride back to where I'm working. If Dutch and Ed've got a notion to stop me, they're sure welcome to try."

"Expect they will. Just like Red and Art Lea, they ain't forgot that day in Waco."

Bill Thompson grinned in his humorless way. "Neither have I," he said and turned for the doorway. "So long."

"So long," Jace Connors replied, "and luck."

9

Thompson, ignoring the wary attention again turned upon him, crossed the saloon floor leisurely. Reaching the entrance, he placed both hands on the batwings as if to make passage of his squat, thick-shouldered figure through the doorway easier. For a long moment he remained there squared against the bright sunlight, and then moved on.

All nonchalance ended there. As the doors swung together, he stepped briskly aside, hearing as he did the quick scrape of chairs and a low rumble of voices which meant but one thing to him: Dutch Reiker and Ed Cherry — possibly a couple others — were going to have their try at him. Immediately he went over to the opposite side of the street, walking with considerable more agility than might be expected of a man so stockily built, and drew up next to an empty store building. There, well in the shadows and out of sight, he waited.

Waco . . . Thompson's thoughts slipped back to that day when, as an express company's special deputy, he, with four other lawmen, stood watch for Red King and his gang. Earlier he had been warned that the outlaws intended to rob the company of a shipment of gold that was being held in the safe for transit the following morning. Red and his bunch planned to move in and, by sheer number, take the gold.

They had made the attempt, but Thompson and the deputies were ready. In the shootout Red's brother was killed along with three other outlaws while the party of lawmen sustained only minor wounds. King had sworn vengeance on Bill Thompson if and when they met again.

The range detective had accepted the threat with his customary philosophical stoicism, never troubling himself to seek out or avoid the outlaw, and when they did come face to face some months later in a Mexican *cantina* in Juarez, he prepared to settle the matter. But King apparently felt the moment was not right, and making a display of indifference, he had turned away and left the saloon, endeavoring to give all who witnessed the encounter the impression that it was something of no consequence.

Thompson knew better. He had dealt with the Red Kings of the frontier all too often to believe that Red was forgoing the promise to avenge his brother. The odds simply hadn't been to his liking; he'd wait for another day, likely one when he'd have more guns backing him. Such was also evident to everyone else in the *cantina,* including Jace Connors, who happened to be present; Red simply had no desire to stand and draw against the range detective, admittedly one of the fastest and most deadly of the professionals.

Thompson pulled back slightly. Dutch Reiker, a lanky, slope-shouldered man with flat, empty eyes, was suddenly standing in the entrance to the saloon. Thumbs hooked onto his gun belt, he swept the street with a lazy, probing glance.

Dutch was alone. Such indicated that Ed Cherry had gone out the back door of the Palace, was probably hoping to locate him and work around to where he was in behind. In that way the two outlaws, if there were but two of them involved, could trap him in a crossfire.

Bill pivoted, dropped back to the rear of the vacant building, and behind it, moved to where he was below the saloon, and then returned to the street. Cherry would now have to circle wide to come at him from the rear, and in so doing, would reveal his position.

He was only a short distance now from

where he'd picketed the buckskin. If he wished, he could continue the remaining few yards, mount up, and ride on, leaving Cherry and Dutch Reiker to vainly search the scatter of buildings for him. But no such thought occurred to Bill Thompson. These were outlaws, and they were looking for a showdown; such was reason enough, and an excuse, to oblige them.

Cherry appeared in a passageway between the general-merchandise store and an empty building that had apparently once housed a feed-and-seed dealer. The man, moving forward along the splintery board wall of the old structure, halted when he reached its front, and removing his hat, made a cautious examination of the street. Seeing no one other than Reiker, he took a further step into the open and gestured to his partner.

At that moment sound on beyond him, near where he'd left the buckskin, came to Thompson. He whirled, the forty-five on his hip appearing in his broad hand as if by magic.

"Marshal —"

The detective swore softly. It was Jim Court. The deputy had evidently seen the buckskin, had ridden on by intending to look elsewhere along the street for him.

Spotting him there at the corner of the old building, he hauled up short — but in so doing, he had drawn the notice of Dutch Reiker and Ed Cherry.

"Keep back — out of this," Thompson warned, and moved into the clear.

Instantly Cherry whipped out his pistol, fired. Haste destroyed his aim and the bullet went wide. Thompson, calm, cool, dropped him with a solitary shot, pivoted smoothly, and drove a bullet into Dutch Reiker just as the outlaw got his weapon free of its holster and was bringing it up.

With the echoes of the gunshots rocking back and forth along the street, bringing forth a dozen or more curious but cautious onlookers from the saloons, Thompson reloaded his weapon. And then with thin, flat layers of powder smoke still drifting about him, he faced Court.

"You looking for me?"

The deputy, stiffly upright on the saddle, face blanked by amazement, was speechless. Finally the paralysis broke.

"I ain't never seen anything like that — shooting so fast and hitting dead center, I mean! Why them two never —"

Thompson, moving up to the younger man, repeated his question. "You come for me?"

Court bobbed, got control of himself. "Yes, sir, Marshal, I sure have. We've got some trouble."

The range detective, without a backward glance to the street, where a considerable number of persons were now crowding around Reiker and Ed Cherry, strode to where the buckskin was standing, and freeing the leathers, stepped into the saddle.

"Can tell me about it while we're riding back," he said as Court spurred up beside him.

The deputy was shaking his head. "Them two gunslingers, was they —"

"Just a couple that figured to try their hand but didn't make it," Thompson replied, dismissing the subject. "This trouble you're talking about, what is it?"

Court settled back into his saddle as they broke clear of the town and started across the flat, and faced the range detective.

"There's a herd trailing up from Texas. Comes through every year —"

"Know who heads it up?"

"Man name of Tom Howard. Real hardcase. Always got a crew of toughs with him, more gunslingers than drovers. Same goes for him. Shot a man down south of here last year who jumped him about some steers he'd glommed on to."

"You mean rustled?"

"Not exactly — leastwise, not the way them two did yesterday. He drives his herd across country and just sort of collects all the stock that happens to be handy when he passes by. McBride and other ranchers around always end up losing fifteen or twenty steers apiece."

"They're branded, aren't they?" Thompson asked, lighting a fresh cigar.

"Sure, but this Howard carries some running irons, changes the brands to match one of his own. The association figures it's lost at least five hundred head to him in the past five years."

"They ever try to do something about it?"

"Charlie Gere did once, almost got himself killed. Howard ain't the kind you walk up to and accuse of stealing your cattle. He'll shoot you quick."

Thompson was silent for several minutes. Then, "Where's he now?"

"Been seen east of here, about halfway across the Panhandle. There's a big spring that forms a good watering pond," Court said, rising in his stirrups and looking back toward Boston. Apparently he saw no one in pursuit, which he evidently expected, and resumed his position. "McBride figures that's where he'll camp tonight."

Thompson nodded, puffed thoughtfully on his weed for a time. "Reckon I'd best pay this Howard a little visit this evening," he said, removing the cigar from his mouth. "You know how to find that spring?"

"Never been there," the young deputy replied, "but Lacey knows right where it is. He's waiting for us at the line shack."

Again the range detective was quiet. His shoulders stirred. "You sure you can't find that spring? As soon handle this myself."

Court grinned. "Yeh, guess you would — and could — but we'd better get Frank. Save a lot of time knowing where to go first off, and I expect you'd like to catch Howard in camp."

"Don't matter too much," Thompson said indifferently, "but I suppose it would be quicker."

10

It was yet some time until sundown when Frank Lacey led Bill Thompson and young deputy Jim Court out of a sandy ravine up onto the crest of a rise. Halting, he pointed to a broad swale nestled in the low hills. A fair-sized pond lay like a shining mirror in its center, and around it, milling restlessly, was a large herd of cattle.

"That'll be Howard's outfit," he said.

Thompson studied the shifting mass of dust-dulled color. A thick pall hung in the air and the bawling of the steers was a constant racket. At the near end of the hollow he could see the chuckwagon where the cook had pulled to a stop and, necessary items unloaded, was getting ready to prepare the evening meal. A half-dozen men squatted nearby, evidently finding it unnecessary to ride herd on the cattle now that water had been reached.

"Ain't been here long," Thompson said, shifting his attention to where the wrangler was moving the spare horses into a rope corral.

"Hour, maybe," Lacey said.

Court clucked softly. "Must be twenty-five hundred head in that herd!"

"Easy — maybe closer to three thousand even," Lacey agreed and turned his attention to the range detective. "How you want to do this, Marshal?"

"Alone," Thompson said.

Lacey grinned at the bluntness of the reply and, pulling off his hat, ran fingers through his hair. The smile faded and he frowned.

"This is one time I don't think you ought to try handling something by yourself. Howard's a bad one. He's already killed three men that stood up to him. And that crew of his, they're cut from the same cloth."

"I'm used to dealing with that kind," Bill murmured.

"Howard's different. You can't talk —"

"Outlaws, rustlers, horse thieves — they're all the same," Thompson broke in impatiently. "They savvy only one thing: the business end of a forty-five six shooter and that's what I aim to do my talking with."

"But you're going up against half a dozen of them. Probably a couple three more around somewhere —"

"So? Nothing takes the sand out of a man quicker than to see a couple of his chums blasted to hell right before his eyes," Thompson said. "Anyways, I'll have you two waiting up here ready to take a hand if I need help."

"Why don't we all just ride down into that camp together?" Court wondered. "Sure would even the odds up a bit."

"One reason — we'd likely not ever reach the camp. If Howard's the kind you say he is, him and his bunch would open up on the moment he seen us coming."

"Figuring us for lawmen —"

"Right. Just you let me go at this my way and it'll all work out."

The young deputy shrugged. "Expect you know best."

"For a fact," Thompson said. "Now, keep back out of sight."

He paused, swept the hollow with probing eyes as if making certain he had missed nothing and had the lay of the land firmly established in his mind. The bawling of the cattle had decreased considerably. Thirsts satisfied, they were now beginning to graze, and from the camp the bantering and laughter of the trail hands came faintly up to the crest.

"I'll give you a high sign when I need

you," Thompson said then and swung the buckskin about.

"Ain't no need fretting over him," he heard Jim Court say to the glumly silent Lacey. "He can more'n take care of himself. Why, back there in Boston, I seen him walk out into the street and shoot down them two hardcases quicker'n a cat can blink an eye, and he give them first crack, too."

The detective grinned slightly as the big buckskin walked slowly down the grade. The two deputies viewed him from vastly different points; Lacey considered him ruthless, a killer, little, if any, better than the outlaws he went after. Jim Court looked upon him as a lawman doing his job and getting it done by whatever means necessary.

He reached the bottom of the hill and, still hidden from view of Howard and his trail hands, continued for a good quarter mile and then, circling to his right, doubled back for the camp. He rode boldly into the open, making no effort to conceal his approach, which was bringing the drovers to their feet as they fixed their attention upon him.

Riding past the chuckwagon and the aproned cook, who eyed him suspiciously, Thompson angled his horse toward the waiting men — five hard-looking individuals who appeared ready to go for the guns hanging on their hips at the smallest provocation. He studied the features of each narrowly for a moment and then fixed his attention on the tall, square-jawed one that he guessed would be Tom Howard.

"You the boss?" he asked as he came to a halt.

"That's me. What do you want?"

"Your name Howard?"

"Yep."

"Been waiting for you to show up. I'm looking for a job."

"You wasted your time, fatty," Howard said. "I've got a full crew and ain't needing no drovers."

"I ain't just a drover — I'm a sort of a specialist," Bill said.

Howard stared, scrubbed at his whiskered chin, and glanced about at his men standing a few paces to one side. "Now, what the hell's a specialist?" he demanded.

"Maybe you'd call me an expert," Thompson said genially. "I don't like bragging, but I can take any brand you can come up with, make it into one you want, and nobody'll ever know the difference."

Howard drew up to his full height. "Who the hell says I'm blotting brands?"

Thompson produced his thin smile. "Why, I reckon just about everybody between your ranch and Dodge City does."

Howard's eyes flared and an angry white line formed along his jaw, and then he grinned. "Well, maybe I do pick up a stray here and there. Every damned drover that's hazed a herd up the trail has. Can't be helped sometimes, and there ain't nothing wrong doing it."

"No, expect there ain't, long as you don't get caught, which sure does happen once in a while. That's my calling, fixing up brands so's you don't get caught."

"Here's your coffee," the cook called grumpily from the small fire he'd built near the wagon. "Come and get it 'cause I ain't carrying it to you."

The men siding Tom Howard did not move, seemingly waiting for some indication from the drover that it was all right. Finally, the big man laughed, bucked his head at Thompson.

"You're all right, Pop — I just maybe could use a hand like you," he said, and motioning to the riders, waved them toward the cook. "Step down. We'll have some java and hash this over a bit."

Thompson swung off the buckskin, let the lines drop to the ground. "Could give you a sample of my work. Reckon you've got a few critters that need fixing."

Howard laughed again. "Do at that," he said, and threw a glance at the chuckwagon. The men had filled their tin cups, were squatting on their heels sipping at the steaming, black brew. "How about a little of that over here, Gimpy? Cup for me and one for my expert friend — I never caught your name, Pop."

"Bill will do," Thompson said, watching the old cook hobble painfully toward them with a container of coffee in each hand.

Tom Howard reached into a back pocket, produced a pint bottle of whiskey. "Always carry a little red-eye on me for nipping purposes," he said, pulling the cork with his teeth. Pouring a small quantity into his coffee, he offered it to the detective.

Thompson shook his head. "Ain't much on mixing. Like my java straight, same as I like my liquor straight. This all the crew you got?"

Howard, the bottle returned to its place in his hip pocket, gently sloshed the contents of the cup about, to perfect the blend. "No, couple or three more out there somewheres seeing to the herd, and then I've got a Mex wrangler. Why?"

"Was just wondering if you'd drove a

herd that big all the way here with only five men."

"Not hardly. Got close to three thousand head out there, which is a few more'n I started with," Howard said, grinning. "Soon's the boys there finish off their coffee I'll have them cut out a couple of them strays that joined up with us and you can show me that sample of your work you was talking about."

"Can tell them to cut out five hundred head," Thompson said quietly. "Ranchers hereabouts figures that's what you've rustled going across their range."

Howard's jaw sagged. "What's that?"

"No need to say it again. I'm a range detective that's been hired to —"

"A goddam lawman!" the Texan shouted, and dropping his cup, reached for his gun.

Thompson drew and fired. The bullet caught Tom Howard in the chest, drove him backwards and down. Cool, the detective wheeled as yells went up from the men near the chuckwagon. Two of them, dragging at their weapons, fell as Thompson triggered his gun twice in rapid succession. Those remaining, filled with the same inclination, hesitated uncertainly.

"That's right, boys," Thompson said softly, finally tossing his cup aside. "Just forget what you're thinking unless you want to die for a dead trail boss."

Raising his free hand, Bill signaled to Jim Court and Frank Lacey, watching from the top of the rise, and then, moving to where Howard lay, he picked up the man's pistol, leveled it at the drovers.

"Want you all to throw your guns off into them weeds — goes for you, too, *amigo*," he added, motioning to the Mexican wrangler hurrying up to investigate the gunshots.

The men complied sullenly. The old cook, one hand gripping the side of his wagon, shook his head.

"I ain't carrying no iron."

Thompson nodded. "Just be damned sure you don't try picking one up," he said, and glanced to the deputies coming in at a fast gallop.

Waiting until they had dropped from the saddle and, with pistols drawn, were moving up to him, he said, "We'll be staying the night here."

"Here?" Lacey repeated, looking at Howard and then at the two drovers sprawled near the chuckwagon.

"What I said. Too late to do much now. In the morning these boys are going to cut out five hundred steers for us — the boss there

106

didn't have time to tell them that, but they know it now.

"Want you to find some rope, truss them up good — all except Gimpy the cook there, so's they won't get any notions about leaving during the night. While you're doing that I'll take a ride out to the herd do a little explaining to the rest of the crew about the changes."

Tossing Howard's pistol onto the pile made by the riders, and reloading his own, Thompson holstered it, bobbed at the cook.

"You get on with fixing supper, Gimpy," he said and transferred his attention to the Mexican wrangler. "Want to find a shovel and bury your friends there. Flies draw mighty fast this time of year."

11

Tom Howard's drovers accepted their lot with a minimal amount of grumbling. Weapons removed, their boss dead along with two of their crew members, they saw little wisdom in further opposing the squat, cold-eyed range detective and his two deputies.

The night passed without incident and shortly before daylight Thompson roused the men, and as soon as the cook had fed them, he set them to work cutting out the prescribed number of steers and heading them west under the control of Frank Lacey and Jim Court.

"What're we supposed to do with the rest of the herd?" one of the riders asked when the job was finished.

Thompson, astride his horse and with the weapons of the drovers slung in a blanket and hanging across the back of his saddle, shook his head.

"Up to you, I reckon. Seems sensible to me to go ahead, finish the drive. Expect you're the one that ought to be in charge, Jackson."

The sandy-haired rider who, Bill had learned, was trail boss under Tom Howard, nodded. "Yeh, seems, but who'll sign the papers? Boss's dead."

"He got some kin back where you came from?"

"Nope, was only himself, running a ranch. You shooting him down like you done —"

"Nobody invited him to rustle cows all the way from Fort Worth here," Thompson cut in. "If he hadn't made a practice of it, he'd be walking and talking right now."

"Talking's maybe what you ought've tried instead of using that iron."

"Been a couple others had that notion, I'm told. Now in the graveyard. You know, same as me, that he wasn't the kind to do any dickering."

Jackson shrugged. "Guess so. What about our guns?" he added, pointing at the blanket.

"I'll drop them off about five miles back up the trail. Wait an hour, then send somebody after them — one man, understand?"

"One man," Jackson repeated sullenly.

"Good. Sure would hate to cut your crew down any smaller'n it already is."

Wheeling, Thompson rode out of the camp and a time later caught up with his deputies. They were having no problems driving the small herd; the cattle had watered and fed, as well as rested through the night, and were now satisfied to move along at a fair pace and make no attempt to break and scatter.

The range detective, taking a place behind the steers, merely waved to Lacey and Court as he did, signaling that all was well. He disposed of the improvised sack of weapons belonging to the drovers at what he figured was a five-mile point, and then around noon, as they were entering a broad flat, they were met by McBride, Clete Potter, and Henry Davidson.

The herd had been spotted by one of the Box M riders who had carried word at once to the rancher. McBride had then summoned his two nearest neighbors and, taking along several cowhands, had hurried forth to meet the returning lawmen. The ranchers were smiling as they swung in beside Bill.

"My boys'll take over," McBride said, waving his riders on toward the cattle. "For hell's sake, how many cows did you make Howard give up?"

"Five hundred," Thompson replied. "That's what I was told you all had lost to him."

"Won't be no less'n that," Davidson said. "He give you much trouble?"

"He's dead," Lacey said, riding up at that moment. "So's a couple of them drovers of his."

"Dead? He put up an argument?"

The detective turned his stolid face to the rancher. "Why do you think I had to kill him?" he asked coldly.

Davidson looked away, sighed. McBride brushed the sweat from his forehead. "Couldn't've expected anything but trouble from Howard. Glad to see there ain't none of you hurt."

"What about the rest of Howard's herd?" Clete Potter asked after several moments of silence. "Heard he was moving close to three thousand head."

"Drovers are taking it on into Dodge, far as I know. What I told them they ought to do when they asked me," Thompson said, and glanced to where Jim Court was narrating an account of the meeting with Howard to Henry Davidson. "Point is," he resumed, "you're getting your stock back and this Howard won't be around to bother you no more."

"That's for certain," Potter said, smiling broadly. "Don't know whether it's been said yet or not, Thompson, but I'll say it now —

111

you're doing one hell of a good job for us. Want you to know it's appreciated."

The detective only grunted.

"Job didn't call for you riding into Boston and shooting up the place," Davidson said abruptly.

Bill drew up slowly, cast a sidelong look at Court. Evidently the young deputy had related more than the encounter with Tom Howard to the rancher.

"Boston?" McBride repeated. "You been over there, Marshal?"

"Yesterday morning. Was having a look-see at the place."

"Seems you done more than that," Davidson said. "Had a run in with a couple of men, shot them down."

"Outlaws — sort of old friends of mine."

Clete Potter nodded approvingly. "Don't see nothing wrong in that!"

"Nothing except it's outside his range — and he could've got himself killed," Davidson snapped. "He went alone."

"Don't let that bother you," the detective said quietly. "Can take care of myself."

"What's bothering me is that we've got trouble enough right here in the Panhandle without you going over to that hellhole and to stir up more!"

Thompson's big shoulders shifted indifferently. "Can get yourself another man any time you ain't satisfied."

"We're plenty satisfied, Marshal, but there's still a lot that you need to be doing right here. For one thing, there's all them nesters that need running off."

"I'll get to them soon as —"

"Seems to me you're nit-picking, Henry," McBride said. "If Thompson had a little personal business he was of a mind to take care of, I can't see the harm. He was still on hand to collar Howard and get back the stock we've lost to him, even collected a little interest, I expect."

Thompson, slumped again on his saddle, facing the ranchers and the two deputies, stared beyond them to where the recovered cattle, being driven by McBride's cow-hands, were moving slowly off into the distance.

"Ain't denying that," Davidson said in his whining, complaining way, "I'm grateful. for what he's done. What I'm saying is that there's plenty that needs taking care of around here without egging on that bunch hanging out in Boston and getting them started nipping at us."

"You got some special problem, Henry?" Potter asked. "More'n what we all got, I mean?"

"It's that Mexican living over on my north line. Helps himself to my beef regularly. I want it stopped."

"You tell the marshal about it?" McBride asked.

"No, ain't had the chance."

"Then it's not right to fault him for not doing something about it. Man can't read your mind, Henry. He needs to be told."

Davidson drew out his bandanna, mopped at his neck and face, and settled back on his saddle. "You're right. Guess I'm sort of worked up. Things ain't been going exactly like they ought around the place and I'm taking it out on the wrong man. I'm asking your pardon, Thompson."

Again the range detective only grunted.

"Know I ought to be more than satisfied — and I am, with what you done about Howard. Losing a couple of cows now and then to that Mex ain't worth mentioning."

"Two or two hundred, it's still rustling," Bill said. "All the same to me. Where'll I find this Mexican?"

"Name's Gurule. Got a shack in a coulee just over the line in Colorado. Now, I ain't exactly positive, but I've got a hunch — had it a long time, in fact — that he's stealing my beef a couple at a time, butchering them, and then hauling the meat into La Junta, where he sells it to the restaurants and the meat markets."

"But you ain't got the proof," Potter said.

"No, already told you I wasn't positive. Put my boys to sort of watching, but Gurule's too smart to let himself get caught. However, I done some checking around in La Junta last time I was there, and what I found out sort of added up to him doing what I figure."

Thompson was quiet for a long minute. Then, "What's your brand?"

"Bar-Cross."

"I'll look into it tomorrow morning. Aim to go back to the shack, get myself a bit of shut-eye now. Was about half awake most of the night."

"Morning'll be fine," Davidson said. "What I'd like for you to do is run up to Gurule's place, watch him for a spell. Then if things don't look exactly right to you, bring him in so's I can have a talk with him."

Bill Thompson nodded. "Can expect to hear from me tomorrow afternoon," he said, and roweling his buckskin gelding, rode on.

12

"I want you to take a ride over to that brakes country south of here," Thompson said as he was saddling his horse that next morning. "Got a feeling something's going on over there that we ought to know about."

Lacey, frowning, said, "That mean you're going over to see this Mexican Davidson figures is stealing his beef?"

"What I had in mind."

"I expect me and Jim had best go along with you. The brakes can wait."

Thompson pulled the forward cinch of his saddle tight about the buckskin's belly, locked it with the buckle's tongue, and tucked in the tag end of the strap. He came about slowly, then faced the two deputies.

"I'm getting a mite tired of you second-guessing me. Happens I'm dealing the cards in this game, and when I want something done, I expect you to do it."

Lacey's features were stiff. "Only thinking about you maybe getting bushwhacked or something."

"Don't. I ain't got to the point yet where I need a nursemaid."

"Not saying you do," the older deputy persisted doggedly, "but Jim was telling me about that ruckus in Boston. Like as not there'll be some of that bunch — friends of them two you cut down — that'll be looking for you."

"Maybe."

"And that's pretty rough country up there. A lot of trees and brush. Man could hide out —"

"Not much you could do about that," Thompson said, tightening the back cinch strap of the big hull and testing its stability. Double-rigged, it had a long tree that was capable of holding the detective's squat bulk comfortably.

Frank Lacey sighed. "Well, it's up to you, of course. Like you say, you're the boss, but you best keep an eye open for trouble — and on Gurule, too. Been told he is a real slick one that'd as soon stick a knife in you as draw a breath."

"Be just one to one, and with them kind of odds there's nothing to fret over," Bill said, raised his glance to the flat west of the line shack. Two riders were approaching. Court and Lacey shifted their attention to the horsemen. The older man squinted into the sunlight.

"Looks like Noah Clevenger. And that's the sheriff — Akins — with him. What do you reckon they want up here?"

Thompson shrugged. "Me, most likely."

Jim Court bristled. "Hell, they ain't got no right coming onto neutral territory!"

"Could be just a social call," the range detective said dryly, and moving away from the buckskin, crossed to the shack. Folding his arms, he leaned against the wall, awaited the arrival of the lawmen.

Clevenger came straight to the subject. As he and his fellow officer drew to a halt on the hardpack fronting the cabin, he fixed his bitter features on Bill.

"Little matter of a killing — three of them, in fact, I want to talk to you about, Thompson."

The detective nodded. "Go ahead."

"Man rode into Clayton last night, said you'd shot down his boss and a couple of trail hands. Then you helped yourself to five hundred steers from the herd they was driving to Dodge City. That true?"

"About the size of it, all right."

"Only it ain't the way that jasper, whoever he was, made it sound," Lacey added. "It was —"

"I'm talking to Thompson," Clevenger snapped. "Was high-handed murder from

118

what I can tell, and I'm taking you back to stand trial for it. Sheriff Akins here'll —"

"No, I don't think so," Thompson cut in quietly. "First place, it wasn't murder. Howard went for his gun, I beat him to it. Same with the two others. They made their try, came up slow."

"That's the truth," Lacey said flatly. "Court and me seen it. We were standing on a bluff, looking down, watching."

"Howard's that Texan that's been coming through here for years, grabbing ever cow he comes across and adds them to his herd," Court said, and pointed a finger at Akins. "The boss's complained to you half a dozen times about him, and you always put him off by saying it's out of your county and you couldn't do nothing about it. Well, the marshal here did."

Clevenger brushed impatiently at his jaw. "Maybe so, but shooting down three men and taking five hundred steers —"

"The steers belonged to the ranchers around here. They was only getting them back — finally. Far as the shootings were concerned, Howard and them toughs he had siding him had their chance."

"Anyway," Lacey said, "I can't see as it's any butt-in of yours, Noah. All took place here in the Strip. You or Akins neither one've got any authority up here."

"Just could be I'll get the authority — if these killings keep on," Clevenger declared. "When there's cold-blooded murder going on somewheres, I think the court can find —"

"Wasn't no murder to it. Was a fair fight."

"That go for those two men he blew to hell over in Tolan's Wash?"

"He give them a chance to throw down their guns and quit. They didn't take it."

"So he dynamited them."

Jim Court bobbed. "Can you think of a better way to get them out of that old house? We could be there yet had we just kept on swapping lead."

Thompson, listening to the exchange, shifted wearily. "Marshal, I haven't killed a man yet that I didn't first offer him the chance to surrender, but I've got something else to do besides wrangle with you. If you want to do some complaining, go do it to McBride and the other members of the association."

"Already have," Clevenger said. "They tell me they're against your killing anybody, that you've been told to bring in any man you catch rustling cattle or stealing horses so's they can be tried. That your understanding?"

Thompson nodded. "Already said this several times — I give them their chance to quit. If they don't want to take it, it's their funeral."

Clevenger spat into the dust. "Sure ain't likely to be yours," he said cynically. "Unless someday one of them gets you in the back."

"Don't stew none about that, Marshal," the range detective said with a half smile. "Time comes for me to die, well, I reckon I'll die. Meantime I'll just go on about my business, doing what I'm paid to do."

Akins, a small, sharp-faced man wearing fringed buckskin, spoke up for the first time.

"Ain't nothing I can do about you here in the Strip, Thompson, but if you ever cross the line into my county I'll throw you in jail so quick you won't know what hit you."

"You'll be needing a charge, Sheriff."

"I'll find one."

"Trumping one up won't work — I know the law. And count on this, any time I've got a need to cross over, or maybe pay a visit to Clayton, I'll do it. Advising you right now, if I ever do, don't go prodding me."

"That a threat?" the lawman demanded, his lean face darkening.

Bill Thompson's shoulders lifted, fell. "Take it any way you please," he said, and pulling away from the side of the line shack, crossed to the buckskin. "We're through jawing far as I'm concerned. I've got work to do."

"Another killing?" Clevenger asked in a cutting, sarcastic tone.

"Reckon that's anybody's guess," the detective said, swinging onto his horse.

"Who'll it be this time?"

Thompson settled himself on the saddle, leveled his cool gaze on the lawman. "Ain't decided yet. Except I'll just have to draw straws, see who's next."

Jim Court laughed. Clevenger and Akins exchanged angry glances.

"Can do without any smart-mouthing," the marshal said tautly.

"And you're wasting my time, something I can sure do without," Bill replied evenly, and shifted his attention to the two deputies. "Don't be looking for me back till after dark," he said, and cutting away from the hitchrack, rode past Clevenger and Akins, and struck northeast across the prairie.

13

No matter where he worked, Bill Thompson thought as the gelding moved steadily away from the line shack, he found himself at cross-purposes with the law. He wished it could be different. He had utmost respect for the job that lawmen, as a whole, did, and there was no good reason why there was not any cooperation.

But it never seemed to pan out that way. His presence always served to antagonize the official lawmen he encountered, and most of them looked upon him as being on the same level as the outlaws they both opposed. Not that he ever lost any sleep over it. The marshals and sheriffs and lesser representatives of the law could take it or leave it, as far as he was concerned. His profession was the apprehension of renegades — usually those the ordinary lawmen, either by choice or by inability, failed to capture. A man would think they'd appreciate his position instead of doing everything they could to hinder him; they were all working toward the same end, but Bill Thompson had long since stopped puzzling over the paradox.

The range detective looked ahead. He was entering a much more broken country — shallow washes filled with sage, rabbit brush, and other spring growth were plentiful, and the grassy flats and slopes of the low hills were pocked with squat cedars and junipers. Here and there were beds of stiffly erect thistle, their feathery flowers a pale lavender in the bright sunlight; and bayonet yucca, with seed pods like miniature brown melons along their center stalks, were at every hand.

"When you see two red buttes, turn due east," Frank Lacey had told him in reply to his request for directions to the Gurule place, and seeing the mounds now, Bill began to veer more to his right. Shortly he came in sight of a long, fairly deep swale. A small grove of cottonwoods grew near its center, and rising from the midst of them was a column of smoke. Gurule's, undoubtedly.

Allowing the buckskin to continue at a leisurely lope, Thompson studied the oasislike area. There appeared to be a bluff to the north of the man's holdings; it offered the possibility of looking down on whatever activity was taking place without being noticed. Accordingly, Bill swung wide, came in onto Gurule's from that side.

He could hear an occasional click of metal as he rode slowly up to the summit of the bluff, and staying in the saddle until the last practical moment, he finally halted, dismounted, and after wrapping the buckskin's lines about the stem of a bitterbush, advanced to the edge of the formation.

Gurule's house, a not too bad arrangement of rock and rough boards, was directly below. It was built close to a spring that bubbled out of the dark soil, formed a narrow stream for a few yards, and then disappeared again into the earth. There was no sign of the Mexican, but the detective could see two dogs asleep at the side of the shack; a team of horses hitched to a wagon had been pulled up under the trees at the edge of the yard.

But more importantly, a freshly skinned steer was hanging by a rope from one of the cottonwoods. On a bench close by were several knives, a meat saw, and a hatchet. He'd come just at the right time; Gurule was in the act of butchering a steer.

At once Thompson dropped back to his horse and, mounting, circled down off the bluff and rode into the swale where the house stood. He'd scarcely come in view of the shack when both dogs, aroused by the sound of his approach, sprang to their feet and charged him, barking furiously. Both were large, thick-necked mongrels that made it clear they would as soon tear him to shreds as not.

Bill drew to a halt, attention on the door of the house. As the dogs raged about the nervous buckskin, he leaned forward, rested an arm on the horn of his saddle, and waited for Gurule to appear. The Mexican came out after a few moments, halting on the small landing below the door.

He was a dark, slim man somewhere in his late thirties, Thompson guessed. He stood motionless for a time, eyeing the detective suspiciously, and then, taking up a rifle propped against the wall of the shack, he whistled in the dogs and advanced to the center of the yard.

"What you want?" he called as the mongrels took up a stand behind him.

"Was passing by, seen your smoke," Thompson said. "Was hoping maybe I could buy myself a meal."

Gurule gave that consideration. Then, "Where you from?"

"Texas — a few other places."

The Mexican mulled that about, finally nodded. "All right, you come in. I sell you grub."

126

Thompson touched the gelding with his spurs, moved deeper into the clearing. Halting beneath one of the larger trees, he dismounted, tied the horse to its trunk, and turning, faced the man.

"Sure a fine place you've got here," he said, glancing about.

Gurule, rifle still in his hands, ignored the comment. "What you want to buy?"

"Jerky, some coffee, and biscuits. Don't need much."

"You pay with hard money?"

Bill thrust a hand into a pocket, rattled the coins he was carrying. His gaze settled on the steer suspended from the cottonwood.

"Looks like you're in the meat business."

"*Sí*," Gurule replied, noncommittally.

"You make a lot of money at it?"

The Mexican shrugged, relaxed slightly. "It is a way of living."

Thompson continued to drift his gaze over the yard. The hide of the steer lay off to one side at the edge of what looked to be a disposal pit.

"You live here alone?"

Gurule's dark eyes narrowed and the rifle lifted slightly. "You ask many questions, *señor*."

"Just wondering," the range detective said indifferently.

The Mexican was alone, he guessed, but he'd take no unnecessary chances. Best to wait until he was certain or was in a position where someone still inside the shack could not take a shot at him.

"Mighty fine-looking beef," he said, moving slowly toward the slaughtered steer. "Prime stuff. You got more stock around somewheres? Don't recollect seeing any on the range when I rode in."

Gurule's thin shoulders stirred. "This beef I buy from a rancher. It is better than to raise my own."

"I see. You buy them one at a time, butcher and sell the meat — or maybe you've got a big family to feed."

"No family. The meat I sell in La Junta. Sometimes in Trinidad."

"Expect you do pretty good at it. Steer cost you maybe twelve, fifteen dollars. I'm betting you collect four, maybe five times that much from the butcher shops."

"Maybe."

"Sure a good arrangement. You don't have to worry about running a herd — just buy a steer, slaughter it, and sell it off when you're needing cash. Sort of like to try the idea myself someday."

"There is no room for another around here," Gurule said hurriedly. "There is land

128

to the west — and more towns where the meat can be sold, many more towns."

Thompson gave that serious thought. Then, "Yeh, I reckon you're right. You've got the fresh-meat business cornered around here. Who'd you say you bought your steers from?"

Gurule's shoulder's moved again. He shifted the rifle to the crook of his right elbow, allowed it to hang.

"There are many — a man named Davidson. His *rancho* — it is not far."

"That where this steer came from?" Thompson asked.

"*Sí.*"

The detective, one of the cottonwoods now between him and the house, guessed he'd heard enough. The lines in his face deepened and a hardness came into his voice.

"Seems you ain't got around to settling up with Davidson for this steer — or any of the others you've helped yourself to. He wants to talk to you about that."

Gurule frowned, stiffened. "I do not understand, *señor,*" he began, shifting the rifle back to a ready position once more.

"Oh, I reckon you do, *amigo,*" Thompson drawled. "And don't get anxious with that gun. You'll never get the chance to use it."

Gurule wagged his head, settled back. "There is a sad mistake," he murmured. Then, "I do not think you are a lawman."

"Don't worry about that — just let the rifle drop and start loading that steer and the hide in your wagon. We're taking a drive over to Davidson's place."

The Mexican shrugged, started to comply with the command. Abruptly he lunged to one side, swung the weapon up, levering a cartridge into its chamber as he did.

"No!" he shouted desperately.

Thompson rocked forward, drew, fired his pistol, all in a single, flowing motion. Gurule staggered as the forty-five bullet drove into him. Muscle reflex triggered the weapon he clutched, but the barrel was already lowering and the slug buried itself in the packed soil.

Still poised, the detective rode out the moments, eyes on the Mexican, pistol leveled for a second shot if it became necessary. Gurule, a hunched shape in the drifting powder smoke, fought to stay upright, but his knees were slowly giving way. Suddenly the rifle slipped from his stiffening fingers and he twisted partly around. The dogs were barking frantically, heads low, hair on their backs bristling.

Gurule sank to his knees, hung briefly,

and then fell forward, sending the mongrels into a new frenzy of rage. Thompson's taut, blocky figure relented. Drawing himself up, he reloaded his pistol, dropped it back into its holster. One more killing for Noah Clevenger to chalk against him, he thought as he turned to fetch the team and wagon.

And he could not expect Henry Davidson to be happy about the way things had turned out, either, but the rancher could be certain of one thing: Gurule was out of the meat business.

It was late in the afternoon when Bill Thompson, on the seat of Gurule's wagon, his buckskin trailing along behind, rolled into Davidson's yard and pulled to a stop at the hitchrack.

He'd loaded the Mexican's body, along with the slaughtered steer and its hide, into the vehicle, covered them with a tarp, and headed out about midday. There had been no one else but Gurule at the house, and the only opposition he'd encountered had been the dogs. He finally quieted them by slicing off two generous portions of meat from the carcass of the steer, tossed the chunks off to the side for them. It had satisfied both, and he'd been able to go about his chores, concluding them by putting a match to the shack and burning it to the ground.

"I've got Gurule here — along with the last steer he rustled from you," Bill said when the rancher stepped out onto his porch. "He's been rustling your beef right along. Found a pit where he's been burying hides."

Davidson nodded. "Knew I was right. Where is he?"

The detective came down off the wagon, pulled the tarp aside. "Right here."

The rancher's mouth gaped. "Dead! Goddammit, Marshal, I said bring him in so's I could talk to him, not kill him."

"Went at me with his rifle when he found out what I was after," Thompson said, moving to the back of the wagon and freeing the buckskin's reins. "Was either him or me."

Stepping up onto the saddle, the range detective settled himself, placed his cold gaze on Henry Davidson.

"Little hard to savvy you fellows up here. You want a job done, but you don't like facing up to it when it is. Now, I want you all to get together, make up your minds how it's to be because I've listened to all the belly-aching about the way I work that I aim to. Can find me at the line shack waiting to hear from you."

14

"They won't be showing up — none of them," Jim Court said that following morning.

Thompson, standing just outside the doorway of the cabin, spat into the dust. Nearby, his horse and those of the two deputies were saddled and bitted, ready to begin the range patrol the detective had planned for the day, but was now delaying.

"You for certain aim to quit?" Lacey asked.

"Same as told Davidson I was. Be more to my liking to stay and finish the job."

"That's what they'll want you to do," the older deputy said. "You're doing what they've been hoping to get done for a long time — only they don't want to admit it or let folks think they sanction your way of doing it."

Thompson nodded slowly, puffing gently on his cigar. "Usually how it is —"

"I agree with Jim. There ain't none of them going to show up, which is the same as saying they want you to keep on working."

The detective made no answer, continued to stare out across the flats. Jim Court, a half-empty cup of coffee in his hand, took a swallow.

"Gurule give you much trouble?" he asked.

"No more'n I expected. Was his damned dogs that got in the way. Both of them meaner'n hell. Had a notion to put a bullet in their heads to get rid of them, then it come to me they were vicious because the Mex had made them that way and didn't know no better."

"What'd you do about them?"

"Fed them. Was all it took."

"Gurule's been a burr under Davidson's saddle blanket for years. Some of the other ranchers've lost stock to him, too — not much, just a little at a time."

"Still stealing, like the marshal says," Jim Court commented.

"Reckon it is," Lacey agreed.

Thompson removed the cigar from his mouth, gave the older deputy a searching look. After a few moments he nodded and, pulling himself erect, moved toward his horse.

"Expect we'd best get started."

A grin crossed Jim Court's face. "That mean you're staying on the job?" he asked, following the squat detective.

"Well, don't look like they're coming. Guess that means they want me to keep on working. That how you see it?"

"Sure is," Court replied, and glanced at Lacey. "That go for you too, Frank?"

"They don't want him to quit," the older man said, and then added to Thompson, "What about taking along a bite of lunch? Said you wanted to spend the whole day looking over the range."

"Won't be needing any," the range detective said, going onto his buckskin. "We can swing by Clayton, get us something to eat at the restaurant."

Both deputies stared at him in disbelief. Lacey shook his head. "I recollect Clevenger and Akins saying —"

"I don't worry none about them," Thompson said with a tight smile on his lips. "No call for you to, either."

They rode out, moving due south for a time, their horses abreast, Thompson utterly silent as was his usual way, the two deputies carrying on a continual conversation between themselves. Occasionally the range detective would veer off, ride to the crest of a rise, and have a long, probing look at the country.

"Smoke coming from a draw over to the west," he said the third or fourth time he'd followed such procedure. "Reckon we'd best see what's going on."

It proved to be the campfire of two drifters. Hunched over their morning meal, blankets still spread out on the ground nearby, they came warily to their feet as Thompson and the deputies rode in.

"This here's private range you're on," the detective said, resting a forearm on his saddle horn and leaning forward. "Expect you know that."

The older of the pair frowned. "No, we didn't. Wasn't doing nothing, anyway — just camping for the night."

"Which way you headed?"

"West. Aim to get to California someday."

"You'd better get moving then," Thompson said, letting his glance shift to the two horses standing off to the side near a cedar. Both were worn, showed the effects of a long journey. "Animals of yours are in bad shape. If you'd kept going for another hour, you'd've come to a spring. Been a better camp."

"Was pitch dark time we got here," the younger man said. "What we was hoping for was a town. Finally give up, stopped here."

"You're too far south for a town," Lacey said, "but if you'll keep riding west you'll come to one."

"Obliged," his partner said, dropping

back onto his haunches again. He glanced up apologetically. "Would offer you some coffee, only this here ain't much — more colored water'n anything. You're welcome, however, to —"

"We just ate," Thompson said, straightening up in the saddle and pulling away. "We'll be back by here later on. Want to find you gone."

"Can bet on it," the older man said, and took up his cup of thin coffee.

"Was a bit easy on them, wasn't you?" Frank Lacey said, as he and Court swung in beside the detective. "Sort of expected you to do some hell-raising."

Thompson eyed the deputy speculatively. "Maybe even shoot them down, that it?"

"Well, maybe not that bad, but . . ."

Bill turned away. "They ain't the kind to be clamping down on. Just pilgrims going somewheres. Had they been setting up housekeeping, it would've been different."

"You going to have a look there later, be sure they're gone like you said?" Court wondered.

"Won't be no need. They won't be there," Thompson said. "That a homesteader down there in them trees?"

"Humboldt's place," Lacey replied. "He's on Lindeman's land. Amos sort of feels sorry for the woman and kids. Old Lew ain't worth a damn himself."

"They living on Lindeman's beef?"

"Nobody ever looked into it to find out. Pretty sure they are."

"Makes them rustlers."

"Yeh, guess so, but I don't figure they ought to be put in the same class as them two we caught in Tolan's Wash or —"

"Why not? They're stealing another man's cows. Makes them rustlers."

Thompson began to slant toward the cluster of shabby buildings crouched in the shade of several cottonwoods growing in the bottom of the swale. Beyond the shacks lay a cleared field, but there appeared to be only a small portion of it near the house that was under cultivation.

"Don't see any spring," the detective said. "They trying to farm without water?"

"Haul in what they need from a sink about five miles up the way. Guess they figured there'd be enough rain to raise a crop — only there never is. Same mistake a lot of squatters made."

Bill said no more and, flanked by the deputies, rode down into the littered, weedy yard of the homesteaders. Several dogs appeared, began to bark noisily. At their outbreak a slatternly woman, hair stringing down around her face and neck, shapeless dress hanging like a drab sack from her bony shoulders, came through the doorway and paused. A half-dozen ragged children appeared, crowded about her, clinging to her skirt. The oldest could have been no more than seven or eight years of age.

"The mister ain't around," she said in a dragging voice before Thompson could speak.

"Where is he, Mrs. Humboldt?" Lacey asked.

At the mention of her name, the woman's belligerent attitude softened. Raising a hand, she brushed at her face.

"Gone over to the pond — fishing, I reckon."

"The Hayden place," Lacey explained in a low voice. "Six or eight miles east of here."

"Hayden — he another squatter?"

"Was a rancher. Died and his family moved on. When he was alive he took a team and a fresno, dug out a spring on his land, made himself a fair-sized pond. Put fish in it for his kids."

Thompson stepped down from his horse, walked toward the scatter of sheds behind the shack. The woman regarded him suspiciously.

"What're you hunting for?"

139

"Hides," the detective said, glancing about. "Ones wearing Lindeman's brand. He's missing cows."

The lips of the homesteader's wife tightened. Bill, ignoring the excited dogs racing about him and yapping at his feet, crossed to one of the sheds, had a perfunctory look inside, transferred his attention then to the yard in general. After a moment he wheeled, retraced his steps to the buckskin.

"No sign of any," he said, leveling his eyes on the woman as he went back onto the saddle. "Want you to tell your mister something for me."

"What?"

"That I've been hired by the Cattleman's Association to stop the stealing that's going on around here. It'll go hard for any man I catch. Now, if you folks are having trouble getting enough to eat, tell him to go ask Amos Lindeman for a steer — and he'll like as not give you one. He ain't going to let you and your kids starve — but your man's not to do no stealing, understand?"

Mrs. Humboldt nodded. "I'll tell him, sure."

"Aim to be coming through here regular, keeping my eye on things. He best not try to fool me."

"I'll tell him," the woman repeated.

Thompson touched the brim of his hat with a forefinger, wheeled the buckskin about, and rode out of the yard.

Before they had reached the edge of the poorly cleared area, Jim Court glanced back. His features were puzzled.

"You for certain there wasn't no hides laying around there somewheres? Everybody knows Lew Humboldt's been helping himself to Lindeman's stock."

"Was one pegged out there behind the outhouse, couple more already dried and stashed under some bushes."

"Then why'd you say —"

"It'll work better this way. Wouldn't've done no good to jump on the woman, but I'm betting she lays the law down to him when he shows up."

"You think he'll go to Lindeman, ask him for a steer when he gets hungry?"

"Hell, they're living on his beef, probably eating it three times a day. All else they've got is a truck garden and it's drying up for want of water. Weeds have all but taken it over, too. She'll make him go to Lindeman all right, or else nag at him till he starts working the place."

"Feel kind of sorry for her," Court said, pulling off his hat and mopping away the sweat on his face.

Thompson nodded. "It's a hell of a life for a woman, looking ahead to nothing but dropping a kid every year and having another mouth to scrounge up a meal for. But you can't let yourself get to feeling sorry for their kind."

"Seems to me that's just what you're doing," Frank Lacey said.

"Hardly. It's just one of them things a man runs up against ever now and then, and has to handle the best way he can. Country's full of them — no-accounts like that husband of hers hanging on to homesteads that ain't worth riding across.

"Best thing that could happen to all of them is for the government to send them back where they come from, make them get some kind of a job. Their kids'll have half a chance to grow up then."

"That place could be made to pay, leastwise to support them if Lew'd go to work at it," Court said.

"But he won't and he never will. War left a lot of them like him with the same idea: that there ain't no use working hard at anything. They're kind of like cripples, figure to just slide along living from day to day, hand to mouth on whatever turns up. Wouldn't be so bad if it was only them, but there's always a woman and a passel of kids rung in on it."

Lacey and Jim Court were silent, giving Bill Thompson's words thought. The younger man finally broke the quiet.

"You in the war, Marshal?"

"Had three years of it," the detective said, and dropped the subject. He glanced at the sun. "About time we was heading for Clayton. Ain't long till dinnertime."

Lacey grinned tightly, slid a look at Court. "You for sure mean that — about going to Clayton?"

"Hadn't of meant it, I'd never said it," Thompson replied gruffly, and swung the buckskin due west.

15

The same disorderly, dust-filled confusion; the same frantic traffic of hurrying pedestrians, rumbling wagons, shying horses and plodding, heedless mules. Bill Thompson, with Lacey and Court siding him, viewed the street with jaundiced eye.

"New towns always look alike," he said as they turned into the restless flow. "Spotted a restaurant when I was here the other day — about halfway along."

Lacey glanced nervously at Court. "Can only hope Clevenger and the sheriff are off somewheres," he said in a low voice, dropping back a step.

The younger man murmured his agreement and added a question. "You figure he's doing this just to show them he ain't scared of them?"

Lacey, waving to an acquaintance shouting a greeting to him from in front of a saloon, brushed his hat to the back of his head.

"Ain't for sure, but I don't hardly think so

because he don't have to prove nothing to nobody. I think he just wanted to come here and eat, like he claims. But we best keep an eye out for the marshal and the sheriff, anyway."

"And for some of that crowd from Boston, too, that're maybe in town. Can bet some of them are looking for him."

If Bill Thompson, the Regulator, was disturbed by that or any similar possibility, there was no indication of it on his broad, stolid face as he led the way down Clayton's single street and drew up before an unpainted store building that bore the sign, RESTAURANT. Dismounting, he waited while the deputies tied their mounts alongside his buckskin, and then, wading through the loose, ankle-deep dust to the doorway of the structure, they entered.

The place was crowded despite the fact it was now well past the noon hour, and charting a course between the dozen or so tables with their assortment of chairs, benches and stools, Thompson led the way to a counter arrangement in the back of the room where a perspiring waitress in a soiled white apron was endeavoring to keep up with the demands of several patrons.

There were only two vacant places at the counter. Thompson signaled Lacey and

Court to be seated and, beckoning to the waitress, took up a stand behind a customer who appeared to be finishing up.

"House's specialty's stew!" the woman shouted above the din.

"That'll do for me," Lacey said.

"Me, too, long as there's coffee to kill the taste," Jim Court agreed.

The humor was lost on the weary waitress. She shifted her attention to the range detective. "Stew be all right with you?"

He nodded, stepped aside to allow the satisfied patron to rise and turn to leave, and settled onto the vacated chair.

"Ain't sure it's worth all this trouble," he said, shifting his attention to the street visible beyond several medium-sized, dust-plated windows in the front wall of the establishment.

"Anything's better'n eating my own cooking," Lacey declared.

The meal finally came — large bowls of sliced potatoes, onions, greens, and chunked beef swimming in a thick soup upon which grease floated in small, irregular circles; uneven slices of still-warm bread, butter, and mugs of steaming black coffee.

"If you want to go around again, just holler," the waitress said, and moved off toward the opposite end of the counter.

"How much you reckon this is going to cost?" Jim Court wondered, starting to work on the stew.

Lacey pointed a spoon at the sign high up on the wall facing him. "One dollar a throw. Can tell you this, once'll be plenty for me. Enough grease in this bowl to fry a side of beef."

"Same here," the young deputy said, and then shook his head. "One dollar — that's a hell of a lot of money just for eats."

Thompson paused, a spoonful of the stew midway to his mouth. "Order up all you want — it's on me," he said, and continued his meal.

A little short of an hour later they were again on the street. Lacey and Court, flanking Bill Thompson, walked with him to the horses, their glances whipping about as they once more nervously sought to locate any source of trouble and circumvent it.

"You all wait here," the detective said as they paused at the hitchrack. "I'm running low on smokes. It'll take me a couple a minutes to buy up some."

He started out into the streaming traffic, looked frowningly over his shoulder at the two deputies as they moved to follow.

"I said wait here. I ain't no wet-eared kid needing a nursemaid," he said, halting them

147

with his tone. "Them horses are more likely to get stole than I am to get shot. You watch out for them, not me."

Lacey and Jim Court turned back, took up positions by the rack, but their attention was on the squat figure of the detective as he shouldered a path through the crowd to the general-merchandise store almost directly opposite.

Entering, he was gone from sight for several minutes, and then once again he appeared, a small parcel in one hand. Giving the street a quick, sweeping survey from the landing fronting the sell-all establishment, he stepped down into the dust and returned to where the deputies waited with the horses. Tucking the package into one of his saddlebags, Bill pulled the reins of the buckskin free of the cross pole, and went onto his mount.

"Reckon we're ready to leave," he said, breaking his tight-lipped silence finally.

Lacey, already aboard his horse, nodded, waited while Court made some adjustment of his gear and climbed onto the bay he was riding. Then, with Thompson leading the way, the deputies maintaining their anxious surveillance, they rode out of the settlement and headed east.

"We had some luck," Court murmured

aside to Frank Lacey. "Akins and Clevenger must've been out of town."

The older man stirred. "Or they were real busy at something," he said with a wink. "Sometimes it's smart to be looking the other way."

Court was staring ahead. "Who's that?"

Four riders had suddenly pulled out of a small grove of trees through which the road led, were stringing across it in a line as if to block passage of Thompson and the deputies.

The range detective, showing no indication that he was even aware of the riders' presence and of the threatening positions they had assumed, continued, slumped indifferently on his saddle, dead cigar butt clamped between his teeth.

"It's Old Man Croft and his sons," Lacey said as they drew nearer. "They'll be looking for trouble, Marshal."

Thompson barely stirred. "Why?"

"They've got a place down on Gere's lower range. Probably heard you aim to run them off."

"Squatters?"

"Yeh, and a real tough bunch. Don't do nothing, just live there in an old tar-paper shack somebody else built years ago. The sheriff figures they're in on some of the stagecoach and bank holdups that goes on around here, but he can't ever catch them at it."

"You think he tries?"

"Guess he does, but they always hightail it for the Strip when they're done, and he can't touch them. Wonder what they've got in mind."

"Whatever, I'll handle it. You just keep back out of the way," Thompson said, and drawing himself erect, spat the cigar butt and settled his attention on the Crofts.

The father, a lean, hawk-faced, bearded man with angry, red-rimmed eyes, raised a hand signifying to halt.

The range detective, spurring slightly forward of the two deputies, drew up.

"You looking to get your head shot off?" he asked bluntly and with no preliminaries.

The question caught Croft unawares. He frowned, slid a glance at his three sons to mask his confusion, recovered, glared at Thompson.

"Maybe you're the one looking for that," he said, and then added, "You're the jasper them cattleman've hired to clean off the range, ain't you?"

"That's me."

"Well, I'm Jared Croft and these here are my boys. One of Charlie Gere's cowhands said you'd be dropping by and telling us to get out. Just aiming to save you the trouble."

"No trouble," Thompson said evenly.

"You're wrong there. You've got trouble aplenty if you figure to run me off!"

"I see," the detective murmured.

Croft's eyes narrowed. He clawed at his ragged beard. "That all you got to say about it? From what that there cowhand said I was expecting you to be some kind of a ring-tailed, stem-winding son-of-a-bitch that'd as soon shoot a man dead as draw a breath. Looks like you ain't nothing but a —"

The blast of Bill Thompson's pistol, coming up magically, stopped the old outlaw's derisive words. He yelled in pain and surprise, clutched his arm, and shouted at his boys. "Shoot him, goddammit!"

The younger Crofts grabbed for their weapons, hesitated as the detective's winter-cold voice reached them.

"Forget it, unless you want to die. I'll kill you — every one of you — right where you're setting if you touch your guns. Just happens I just had my dinner and I ain't in a killing notion; otherwise your pa'd be dead right now instead of having a busted arm."

Old Man Croft, cursing steadily, left hand clamped to his wound, stared at Thompson. "This here's going to get you killed, not us," he said, grinding out the words. "My boy's'll run you down and —"

"They ain't even going to start," Thompson cut in quietly. "Neither are you. By this time tomorrow I want you and your pups off Gere's range and clean out of the Panhandle. If you ain't, you're good as dead."

Croft continued to glare, seemingly unable to comprehend the abrupt turn of the situation. He spat, again clawed at his tobacco-stained beard.

"I ain't sure you're big enough to —"

"Always glad to oblige a man who's got his doubts," Thompson said mildly, and lifting a hand, motioned to Jim Court and Frank Lacey. "You two just pull off to the side there and stay out of this. Seems these jaspers need some convincing that I mean what I say."

"Pa," one of Croft's sons began uncertainly, "maybe we best move on."

The detective smiled bleakly. "Better listen to your baby boy, Pa, unless you want him and you and his brothers to wind up dead right there and now. He's showing sense."

Croft's stare broke. He looked around helplessly, wagged his head. "Yeh, maybe we best. There'll be another time."

"Not around here," Thompson snapped.

"Get that straight in your head, old man. You're moving on. I'll be having a look at that shack where you're holing up tomorrow. If you're still there, I'll kill you."

Croft made no reply, and for a long breath there was only a tense hush in which the only sound was the far-off mourning of a dove. Finally another of the sons spoke.

"Come on, Pa, we've hung around this part of the country for quite a spell. Let's head out for Arizona, like we've been aiming to do."

The old man shrugged. "Yeh, I reckon we might as well," he mumbled, and eyes down, his sons following closely, he swung wide of Thompson and the deputies and rode on toward Clayton.

The detective, reloading his pistol, slid it back into its holster. Casting a look at the departing Crofts, he selected a fresh cigar from his case, thrust it into his mouth.

"Come tomorrow," he said, "I want you to take me over to that shack they've been living in."

Lacey laughed. "They won't be there, you can bet on it."

"Got no doubts myself," Thompson said, roweling the buckskin and putting it into motion, "but I always like to make sure."

Jim Court swore softly. "I ain't ever seen a

man that could draw and shoot as fast as you can, Marshal. That day in Boston and now here, looking at them four hardcases — I don't think there's another man alive that would've dared doing what you did."

"My business and I'm good at it," the range detective said with no false modesty. "Have to be or I'd been dead a long time ago."

"Takes a hell of a lot of nerve," Lacey said.

"Takes more'n that. Man has to keep his mind set on what he's doing."

"Expect any man in a shootout does that," Frank persisted, "and there's still plenty of them get their heads blowed off."

"If they was good in the first place, it was because they had something else in their mind that was nagging at them. If you want to stay alive, you don't ever think of anything else at a time like that except drawing and shooting. If there's something gnawing at you, it'll get you killed."

"Concentration — I reckon that's what they call it," Jim Court said. "Can't let anything break it."

Thompson fired a match, held it to the end of his cigar. "That's a four-dollar word and I ain't sure what it means, but if you say it fits, I'll believe you. Now, there's something else we better do tomorrow. Seen a lot of dust to the east when we was riding to Clayton. Want to have a look — see at what was raising it."

"Could be another herd moving through," Lacey said.

"Yeh, it's a mite late for it, and it could be," Thompson agreed, "but we best be sure."

16

There were no signs of life at the shack where Croft and his sons had been living when Thompson and the deputies rode by that following day. The old outlaw had deemed it wise to heed the Regulator's warning and moved on. Thompson motioned to Jim Court.

"Put a match to it. Don't want nobody else moving in."

The young deputy stepped down from his horse and, piling several dry weed clumps, paper, and bits of trash against a wall, set fire to the accumulation. The tinder-dry boards and their curling, ragged covering smoked thickly for several moments, burst suddenly into crackling flames, and reduced the shack to charred embers in only minutes.

"Dust I mentioned seeing was due east of them buttes," Thompson said as Court resumed his saddle. "Anything special over that way — say, eight, maybe ten miles?"

"Brakes country," Lacey said. "Won't be

somebody with a herd. Drovers stay clear of there — too easy to lose stock."

"Any ranches?"

"Nope. Expect you'll find a couple of squatters."

"Guess that makes it worth looking into," the detective said, and swung away from smoldering remains of the shack.

They came upon the trespassers before reaching the rough, broken area where Thompson had noticed a dust cloud. The first, a man and a woman were loading a wagon with household goods they'd removed from a lean-to canvas arrangement. They'd gotten the word that their presence on the range was unwelcome from a passing cowhand, were moving.

"Ain't no chance of ever making it at farming, anyway," the man said.

Frank Lacey nodded understandingly. "Best thing you can do. This here's cattle country. Man only breaks his back trying to grow crops."

"Can see that now, couldn't at first. Anyways, I'm done. Which way's the closest town where I might find myself a job?"

"Clayton — on west of here," Lacey said, and turned to Thompson. "You want this'n burned down, too?"

The range detective bobbed. Lacey came

back around to the homesteader and his wife. "You got everything out you're aiming to take?"

The man glanced about. "Reckon I have," he said, and moved off after his wife, already climbing onto the overloaded wagon. Taking his place beside her on the seat, the defeated homesteader watched moodily as the deputy started the flames leaping through the crude shelter, and then clucking to his team, swung about and headed west.

"There any more like them along here?" Bill asked Lacey.

Jim Court said, "There's an old line shack on south a piece. Pretty sure there'll be somebody living in it."

The young deputy's assumption was correct. They found that two men had taken over the small cabin. Lacey shook his head in his cautious way as they drew near.

"Place is over the border — in Texas. Ain't much we can do, legally."

"Maybe they don't know they're in Texas," Thompson said, and riding up to the shack, ordered the pair to move on.

Both men, looking to be of the same calling as the Crofts, stood their ground.

"You the law?"

"What I've been told," Bill replied coldly. "Now, you going peaceful — or dead?"

The squatters studied the range detective's grim features briefly, exchanged a quick glance, and turned at once into the shack. Gathering up their belongings and stowing them in a gunnysack, they mounted their horses and rode off to the south.

Thompson waited until they were lost to view in the low hills and the shack was burning merrily, then he spurred up out of the hollow onto the flat above, his gaze now on the country to the east. There was a faint, thin haze of tan hanging in the sky, one much less pronounced than he'd noted before, however. He pointed it out to the deputies.

"About where I seen that dust yesterday, only it ain't moving and it ain't as thick. My hunch is somebody's drove a herd into a big arroyo or box canyon and's holding it there. You think they could do that?"

"Easy," Frank Lacey said. "Hills are bigger and the arroyos are plenty wide and deep. But you won't find no regular trail boss down in there. It'll be somebody wanting to hide out."

"Let's take a look," Bill Thompson said, and put his buckskin into a lope.

As they drew nearer, the dust cloud became denser, took more definite shape. It hung above a long string of red-faced bluffs that angled to the northeast.

"That be in Texas, too?" Thompson asked, raising his voice so as to be heard above the thud of their horses' hooves.

Frank Lacey gave the country a sweeping look as he located his landmarks. "Nope, don't figure it is."

Thompson grunted, satisfied. Lacey, grinning at Jim Court, said, "You reckon it would've made a difference if it was?"

The young deputy laughed. "Not a damn bit."

They rode on, the range detective pulling out a length or two ahead of his companions, round face intent, thick shoulders hunched forward in his customary slouch. Once he removed his hat, ran fingers through his hair, and scrubbed away the sweat from his forehead with the back of a thumb; but never once did his attention waver from the row of bluffs. It was as if he feared he would lose direction and was taking no chance on such occurring.

A half mile short of the apparent arroyo Thompson slowed the buckskin to a walk, allowed the deputies to draw up alongside him.

"We go quiet from here on," he said. "Sure don't want to scare nobody off."

They continued at the slower pace, reached the foot of a gradually rising slope that led to a rim overlooking the cut or whatever lay beyond. The range detective did not halt and dismount but started the buckskin up the grade. He glanced over his shoulder at the deputies.

"Too hot to walk," he said. "Can pull in when we get on top."

Lacey nodded his understanding, said, "Just noticed something — there ain't no bawling going on like we'd hear if it was cattle."

"Means horses then," Court said.

Thompson withheld his opinion, guided the gelding on toward the crest of the rise to where he was but a few yards below it. There he halted, ground-reined the big horse, and cautioning Court and Lacey, walked the remainder of the distance. Squatting, hat off, he looked down.

They were on a row of similar bluffs opposing those they had seen from the flats. Between lay a wide arroyo, both ends of which were blocked by brush fences forming an effective corral. Inside the enclosure was a large herd of horses.

"Must be a couple of hundred in there," Lacey said in a low voice. "Horse thieves, you reckon?"

"Maybe," Thompson replied.

Jim Court pulled himself forward for a

better look. "Them ain't just ordinary broomtails. Could be a bunch that's being drove to Dodge or someplace for selling."

"Hell of a place to be holding a herd. Ain't no water anywheres close," Lacey said. "You see anybody around?"

Thompson pointed to a thick clump of cedars just outside the wall of brush at the upper end of the arroyo.

"There. Three men stretched out in the shade. Must be waiting for somebody."

"Sure a funny place to be doing business if they're dealing in horses," Court said. "I'm betting they've stoled the whole bunch."

"Like as not," Thompson said, pulling back. He was silent for several moments, gaze reaching out across the land across which they had just come. "Reckon all we can do is go down there and find out."

Both Lacey and Court smiled, pleased with what they had heard. The younger deputy said, "You want us with you this time, Marshal?"

"Might as well come along," the detective said. "Only just stand back and let me do the talking. We're playacting at being horse traders, and I'll do the bargaining."

17

As Bill Thompson and his deputies dipped down into the arroyo at a point above the improvised corral, the three men dozing in the shade of the cedars sprang erect. All reached for their guns.

Thompson threw up both hands, palms forward. "Whoa! Whoa!" he yelled. "Ain't no call for that. You're the fellows wanting to sell horses, ain't you?"

The men relaxed. The small, dark member of the trio, evidently the spokesman, nodded slowly. "Yeh, reckon we are. Who're you?"

The range detective, with Court and Lacey at his side, rode in closer. Thompson, eyes reaching beyond the cedars and the brush fence as he made a quick survey of the horses, drew to a halt and swung off the saddle.

"We're the Smith brothers," he said genially. "Who might you be?"

"General U. S. Grant," the dark-faced one said, "but I ain't. Name's Luke Rinehart." He jerked a thumb at his two partners, still poised and suspicious, behind him. "Kid there's Buck Milligan. Other'n's Al Lester."

Milligan was young, had round, blue eyes, an empty face, and a shock of cotton-white hair. Lester, somewhere in his middle thirties, was a lank, hunched individual. All wore shotgun chaps and the pistols hanging on their hips looked as if they had seen considerable use.

"Where'd you hear about us having some horses to sell?" Rinehart asked. He, too, was not fully convinced and continued to regard Bill and the deputies with a narrow wariness.

"Didn't hear," the detective said as Court and Lacey took up a stand near him.

"Then how the hell'd you —"

"Seen your dust," Thompson explained in an easy, offhand way. "Knew there wouldn't be no cattle moving through here and figured it had to be a big bunch of horses on the way to Dodge. That where you're headed?"

Rinehart's tense attitude began to relent. "Maybe," he said. "You looking to buy horses?"

"Always interested if the price is right."

"Price is right long as it's cash," Rinehart said. "Only way we deal — spot cash."

"Sure the best idea, all right," Thompson agreed, gaze again on the horses. "How you getting water and feed to them animals? Don't see no spring and there sure ain't no grass growing in that sand."

"They're doing just fine," the tall Lester drawled. "You tend your dickering, we'll take care of them jugheads."

"Don't want no scrubs," Thompson said, frowning. "Army won't buy them."

Luke Rinehart's attention sharpened. "The Army — that who you're doing the buying for?"

"Ain't saying yes and I ain't saying no," Bill answered with a sly wink. "Mind if we have us a closer look?"

Rinehart shook his head, pivoted, and led the way to the barricade thrown across the upper end of the arroyo. Thompson and his deputies followed, but Lester and Buck Milligan hung back, preferring to wait in the shadow of the cedars.

Halting at the fence, Thompson brushed back his hat, studied the horses minutely. Most of what he could see were branded, and there was an assortment of marks.

Turning to Lacey and Jim Court, he said, "Ain't a bad-looking bunch. Few scrubs in there, but we can cut them out when we get down to trading." He shifted his attention to Rinehart. "How many head've you got in there?"

"Two hundred, give or take a few. How many you interested in buying?"

"All of them."

Rinehart's face reflected his pleasure. "Reckon we can go for that. Sort of promised some of them to a buyer up Kansas way, but there wasn't no handshake agreement. As soon sell them right here."

Thompson, seemingly lost in deep thought, came about slowly, his glance covertly touching Milligan and Lester. Finally he nodded to Rinehart.

"Can get down to business then, but first off I'd like to see the papers on them branded ones."

Luke Rinehart's jaw hardened. Raising a hand, he beckoned to the young blond and the lanky Al Lester. Both came forward at once, moved in beside him.

"Gent here's wanting to see our papers —"

Lester's eyes narrowed. He folded his arms across his chest, squared himself. "One of them particular birds, eh? Always needing to have things down in writing."

"Ain't nothing wrong with that," Thompson said quietly. "Just proves you ain't horse thieves. No point in getting riled, unless you are."

A tense hush fell over the men. Back in the

center of the corral one of the horses set up a disturbance, squealing and kicking and stirring a boil of dust into life.

"You know what?" Rinehart said, breaking the calm as he turned to his partners, "I got a feeling these jaspers ain't wanting to buy horses a'tall. I'm laying you odds they're the law."

The dark-faced man stepped back suddenly. His hand darted for the pistol at his side. In the next fragment of time he staggered back, weapon only partly out of its holster, as Thompson's bullet drove into his chest. Cool, the range detective pivoted, his gun leveling on Milligan and Lester — both frozen, hands spread and well clear of their weapons.

"No, Marshal!" Frank Lacey yelled.

Thompson hung motionless for a long breath, finger on the trigger of his forty-five and ready to press off a bullet.

"No sense killing them," the deputy continued. "Can take them back, let the law hang them."

The range detective's taut, blocky figure relented. His shoulders came back slowly as he lowered his gun. The lines drawn tightly in his face softened and the blankness faded from his eyes. Easing the cocked hammer of his pistol back into place with a thumb, he punched out the spent cartridge, reloaded the cylinder.

Lacey, his weapon drawn, crossed to where Lester and Milligan stood motionless and relieved them of their weapons. "Scrounge up some rope, Jim," he called to Court. "We best tie them up."

The younger deputy wheeled, hurried toward his horse. Lacey faced Thompson, his expression apologetic.

"Figured that was best, Marshal. We ain't even for sure they stole those horses — only looks that way."

Thompson only shrugged.

"Sure hated yelling at you, but you'd a killed them both, I know. You'd a triggered that iron of yours before you seen they wasn't even aiming to draw."

Bill Thompson still made no reply. That he was displeased by the deputy's interference was evident, but whatever he intended to say about it was being passed up, or would come out later. He glanced around as Jim Court, carrying two short pieces of rope, returned, watched in silence while the young deputy began to tie the outlaw's hands together.

"This here's a big mistake — we ain't horse thieves," Lester declared. He was apparently taking his cue from the possibility of doubt as to their guilt that Lacey had expressed. "We bought them horses, every damn one of them 'cepting a few mustangs."

Lacey's shoulders stirred. "Then why'd your partner go for his gun? Innocent man wouldn't've done that."

"Luke probably figured, same as me and Buck did, that you was horse thieves and was aiming to take the herd away from us."

"He's right, mister," the young blond said. "We ain't done nothing wrong."

Lacey slid a glance at Thompson. A hard grin, almost a sneer, twisted the range detective's lips. The deputy, seeing that Court had finished, holstered his gun.

"That'll be up to a judge and jury in Clayton to decide that," he said.

"Hell, that'll mess up the deal we got waiting for us in Dodge!" Lester protested. "We all worked mighty hard getting that herd together — put our life's savings into it, in fact. You take us in to some judge and we'll lose out altogether — everything. Time we can get back here the herd'll be gone, scattered from hell to breakfast."

Lacey gave that thought. Buck Milligan, his youthful features showing anxiety and strain, said, "Why'n't you just let us go? We'll drive the horses on to Dodge, then come back, turn ourselves in to that judge you're talking about. You can even come with us if you're of a mind."

"Reckon we could do that," Lacey said thoughtfully, and glanced at Thompson. "You see any harm in doing what he says, Marshal?"

"Appears you're running this," the detective replied indifferently. "But for my money you're a damn fool."

"Why? If we're wrong —"

"We ain't," Thompson cut in bluntly.

"How can you tell for sure?"

"Reckon I just know," the range detective said and pointed a stubby finger at the outlaws. "You two, march over there to your horses and climb aboard — your bleating don't mean a goddamn thing to me. Look after them, Jim, and don't be scared to use your gun if they try anything," he added to Court.

Attention again on Lacey, he said, "And since you're feeling softhearted about this bunch, you best bring over Rinehart's horse and load him across the saddle so's you can haul him back for a nice church burying. Far as I'm concerned he can keep laying right where he is. The buzzards and coyotes'll tend to him."

Lacey's features were pale, taut. "He's a man, deserves —"

"He's a damned outlaw — trash — and he don't deserve nothing," Thompson broke in harshly and started to move back to where his horse waited. Abruptly he paused, glanced over his shoulder at the deputy.

"One thing I best say now, Lacey — don't you ever butt in on me again when I'm doing my job. That clear?"

Frank Lacey nodded. "It's clear," he said, and followed the detective across the sandy arroyo to Jim Court and the outlaws, mounted and ready to ride.

18

Late in the day they reached McBride's. The rancher immediately sent a half-dozen riders to release the corralled horses and drift them to the nearest water hole, where they could drink and graze. He also sent word to members of the association, calling for them to meet at the line shack the next morning where a decision could be made as to what should be done with Al Lester and Buck Milligan.

Shortly after eight o'clock the ranchers gathered in front of the cabin, and Lacey brought out the two prisoners for the men to see and talk with, explaining how the two maintained they were innocent and begged for permission to continue on to Dodge City with their herd — under guard, if so desired — where they could complete their business transaction and salvage their investment. Charlie Gere put a quick end to the narration.

"That ain't nothing but a crock of bull," he stated flatly, and pointed at Lester. "I seen a wanted dodger on him in the sheriff's office no more'n a month ago. He's wanted for rustling and horse stealing."

Henry Davidson stepped up to the tall outlaw, considered him coldly. "That the truth?"

"I ain't saying nothing," Lester replied.

"What about him?" Lacey asked, indicating Buck Milligan.

"Don't recollect seeing anything on him," Gere said. "Lester's partner was a skinny-looking fellow with dark hair."

"Was Rinehart all right," Lacey said, and glanced at Thompson. "You were right all along, Marshal. Just how I ain't sure."

"When you deal with their kind long as I have, it comes natural," Thompson said, his manner with the older deputy still stiff.

McBride glanced questioningly about at the other association members. "Guess it's settled then. Next thing's to trot them into Clayton, turn them over to the sheriff. He can hold them for trial, and in the meantime put out the word for anybody missing horses to come claim their brands. Expect you'd better do that, Marshal — you and one of the deputies if you like. We want to make damn sure they get there."

Thompson nodded, stared out across the flats. "It make any difference to you if I take them to La Junta?"

The rancher's thick, gray brows came up. "No, why?"

"Just a notion," the detective said, his shoulders twitching. "I need a reason?"

"La Junta'll be a better idea," Frank Lacey said, throwing a quick look at Jim Court. "Won't make any difference. Sheriff up there'll have the same wanted posters as Akins."

"Well, I don't see as it makes a goddamn bit of difference where he takes them long as they end up swinging from a rope," Gere declared. "If the marshal wants to take them there, let him."

"I agree," Amos Lindeman said.

"I ain't disagreeing," McBride protested. "I figure it's up to him. He's the marshal. Was only wondering why. When do you want to head out?" he added, turning to Bill.

"Pretty quick."

"Good. Sooner they're off our hands and behind bars in the calaboose, the better. Who's riding with you?"

"Jim Court."

The young deputy grinned with pleasure at being chosen. Frank Lacey studied Thompson's impassive features for a moment, nodded.

"You'll be needing a bite of grub" he said,

and turned back into the shack. "I'll throw it together for you."

McBride rubbed his hands briskly, again glanced around. "Everything settled then?"

Davidson and Lindeman bobbed their agreement. Gere smiled broadly at Thompson. "Hired hand of mine told me about your little set-to with the Croft bunch. Mentioned a couple other shacks that'd been burned to the ground."

Bill said, "Yeh," in his usual uncommunicative way.

"I'm beginning to think we can clean this country up real quick after all. Don't mind saying I had my doubts there for a spell."

"I'm sure seeing an improvement," Davidson said. "Want you to know we're all standing behind you, Marshal. You run up against anything you don't feel's right, go ahead and do what you figure's necessary."

"He's speaking for all of us, the whole association," McBride confirmed. "Far as we're concerned you've done proved you know best how to handle these outlaws and nesters."

Frank Lacey appeared in the doorway of the shack, a partly filled flour sack in each hand. Stepping out onto the hardpack, he passed them to Court.

"Grub and the stuff to do your cooking

with," he said. "Ought to easy hold you till you get back, but if you run short of anything, buy up what you need in La Junta."

"You be wanting a packhorse?" McBride asked.

Court glanced at Thompson. Bill shook his head. "Can hang them sacks across your saddle."

The young deputy turned to his horse and, knotting the muslin bags together by their slack, draped them over the back of his hull.

"Be needing blankets — and you best fill your canteens," Lacey reminded him.

Court immediately hurried into the shack, returned shortly with the mentioned articles, which he added to the gear of the four horses.

"Can move out any time now," he announced when the chore was finished.

Thompson bucked his head, turned to Milligan and Lester. Leaving their hands tied behind them, he jerked them to their feet and roughly shoved them, cursing and stumbling toward their mounts. Recovering balance, the outlaws waited until Court, and Lacey, stepped up and assisted them onto the saddle. They settled back then, angry, burning eyes on Bill Thompson as he attached lead ropes to the bridle rings of their horses and handed them to the young deputy.

"You'll be riding out ahead, trailing them," the range detective said, seemingly irritated by what he apparently considered a lot of unnecessary trouble. "I'll be right behind you." He pivoted slowly, crossed to his buckskin, and swung heavily onto the leather. Cutting about, he kneed the horse in close to the outlaws.

"I'll warn you one time — you make a wrong move and you're dead, so best you watch yourself. Let's go, Deputy."

He paid no attention to the ranchers and Frank Lacey as the small procession — Jim Court in the lead, followed by the two outlaws and connected to him by ropes, and with him bringing up the rear — moved away from the shack.

Nor did any further words pass between him and the deputy until an hour later when they were riding slowly across a sandy wash. Then, as they reached its opposite bank, the range detective pulled in beside the younger man.

"Keep bearing straight," he directed.

Court stared at him, surprised. "Got to start veering left for La Junta."

"Know that. We ain't going there — leastwise, not right off."

"Then where we going?"

"Boston," Thompson said. "Aim to spend the night there."

19

At Bill Thompson's words Al Lester's head came up, interest breaking on his browned face. But he said nothing, and the range detective, watching the outlaws covertly, grinned faintly. Lester had friends in Boston; that was good.

"Bit risky going there, ain't it, Marshal?" Court said. "Not quarreling with your judgment, but after that ruckus the other day, I'm wondering . . ."

"Don't," Thompson cut in. "Just let me do the figuring."

They reached the small settlement late in the day after a leisurely journey across the low hills and plains. Thompson had been in no hurry, had even stalled a bit now and then under the pretext of resting the horses, which, in truth, fared very well without the occasional interludes.

Boston appeared no different from what it had upon his first visit. The street was deserted except for a few horses standing at the saloon hitchracks and a solitary dog moving indolently along the dusty passage-way lying between the general store and its adjacent neighbor.

"Ain't no jail here," Court observed as they drew up at the edge of the settlement — almost at the identical spot, the deputy noted, where he had halted and watched the range detective shoot it out with two out-laws.

"Won't bother us none," Bill said. "We'll just find us an empty building that's been boarded up, stash these jaspers inside, then have us a time till morning."

Court studied Thompson closely. He seemed to be a different man — light-hearted, cheerful, the direct opposite of his usual quiet, near-sullen self.

"Let's take a pass down the street. Keep your eyes peeled for a building like I talked about."

Surprise again rolled through the young deputy. "Right down the middle — in the open? Ain't you . . ."

"Scared of somebody taking a potshot at me? Ain't likely — not right off," the detec-tive said. "And while we're doing some jawing, I want you to do just what I tell you — and when I tell you. I got a liking for you, boy. That's the reason I picked you to come along instead of Frank Lacey.

"Now, you keep your lip buttoned tight, and when I holler frog, you jump. Time this here's all over you'll still be alive and kicking and you'll've learned a few things about being a lawman — if that's what you're aiming to be."

"What about us, Marshal?" Buck Milligan wondered. "If you've come here to settle a grudge, we sure don't want to get caught in the middle of it."

Thompson considered the outlaw with a half smile. "It make a difference to you how you die?" he asked, answering a question with a question. "You're going to hang when we get to La Junta. Don't seem likely that getting yourself killed here with a bullet ought to bother you none."

Roweling his horse lightly, Thompson moved out into the street, motioning as he did for the deputy, with Al Lester and Milligan trailing behind him, to move up beside him.

As they walked their mounts leisurely through the deep dust, Thompson, slumped on the saddle, his squat shape dark and blocky-looking in the fading afternoon light, let his eyes whip back and forth. He did not miss the blurred faces behind the streaky glass of a window observing their passage, or the sharp attention of three men suddenly standing in the entrance to the Palace Saloon or of two others who came from the shadowy interior of the livery stable, paused in its wide doorway to watch him and his deputy and their prisoners with critical interest.

"Place back up the way looked to me like it'd do just fine," he said as they reached the end of the street and began the return trip. "Was across the street from that saloon — the Palace. Used to be a saddlery, so the sign says."

"I seen it," Court said. "Windows were all boarded up, door was standing open."

"That's the one," the detective said, and angled the buckskin for the sagging hitch-rack at the side of the old structure.

Pulling to a stop, he assisted the deputy in getting the outlaws off their horses and leading them back to the front of the building, where he pushed the pair roughly through the doorway into its gloomy depth. Glancing about, Thompson located a crude bench, the last of the furnishing left in the saddle shop, and pointed to it.

"Set yourself on that," he directed. "It's going to be your bed for the night."

Lester muttered under his breath, crossed to the bench, and sat down. Buck Milligan took a place beside him. Thompson turned to Court. "Give me them ropes you used to tie their feet."

The deputy hurried back to the horses, returned quickly with two short lengths of rope. The deputy, without waiting for Thompson to speak, knelt before the outlaws and secured their ankles.

"We going to have to stay here all night like this?" Lester demanded. "Can't hardly move."

"You'll live through it," the range detective said. "You get tired of setting, stretch out on the floor."

"What about something to eat?" Milligan asked. "Getting on to suppertime."

"Have to wait for morning. Ain't been long since you had some grub."

"Ain't no way of locking this door — only a hasp on it," Jim Court said from the saddlery entrance. "Reckon we'll have to bed down with them."

"Sooner sleep with the hogs," Thompson said dryly. "Run over there to that general store, see if they've got some kind of a lock."

Court was back in only a few minutes. "He ain't got nothing — no kind of a lock. Man there just laughed at me when I asked him. Said a lock'd do no good around here, anyway. Anybody wanting in a place'd just shoot it off."

Thompson shrugged. "Expect he's right," he said, and reaching down, picked up a small stick of wood. With his knife he whittled it into a cylinder of proper size, handed it to the deputy. "Can put this in the hasp. It'll keep the door shut so's the prisoners won't get out."

"From the inside, maybe," Court said, "but what about the outside? Some jasper coming by could pull out the peg, open the door."

The detective rubbed at the stubble on his chin. "Sure could, all right, but they'd be interfering with the law, was they to help a prisoner to escape. I don't reckon there's anybody around here that'll be that foolish."

Wheeling, Thompson crossed to the door and stepped out into the open. Jim Court, clearly unable to understand the Regulator's attitude but unwilling to question him, followed. Pulling the door shut, he closed the hasp, wedged the wooden peg into its throat.

"Best we see to the horses next," Thompson said, starting for the rack.

"Was a livery stable down at the end of the street."

"Won't be using it. There's an old shack at the edge of town near where you met me the other day that'll do. After we water them at

184

the general store's trough, we'll tie them out back of it. Plenty of grass for them to graze on."

Still voicing no questions, the young deputy halted at the hitchrack beside Thompson, and together they led the horses to water. After the animals had taken their fill, the men moved on to the rear of the abandoned building mentioned by the detective, the last structure along the way and at the edge of the town.

When that was done, Thompson, making no explanation of his actions, walked back into the street. He was in an expansive mood, and now, with a fresh cigar clamped in a corner of his mouth, he stood in the open, the last of the sunlight outlining his squat figure, and gave the settlement a thorough surveillance.

Two men had come out of the Palace, were studying him intently. He seemed not to notice, and when Jim Court, delaying briefly with the horses for some cause or other, joined him, he laid an arm across the younger man's shoulder and started for the small saloon a few doors below the Palace.

"What say we have ourselves a snort or two of red-eye before supper?" he said.

Court bobbed. "Could sure use it, but that other place looks like a better —"

"Just as soon stay clear of there," Thompson replied. "Got some old friends running it and I ain't wanting to meet up with them just yet."

Jim Court had reached the point where he could restrain himself no longer. He came to a stop, faced the detective.

"Marshal, what the hell's this all about — you deciding to come here where you're sure to run into trouble instead of heading straight for La Junta. And now putting those two horse thieves in a shack where they're bound to get turned loose —"

"Don't get you dander up, boy. It'll all come out in the wash. Right now let's get that drink, then we'll go have us a big supper."

"Supper — where? There ain't no restaurant."

Thompson pointed to the two-story, ornate residence at the end of the street. A woman in a bright orange dress had come out, was sitting on the railing that surrounded the porch.

"Be doing our eating with the ladies there. Can get ourselves a room for the night, too. Whether you do any sleeping or not's up to you, but you enjoy yourself, Deputy. I'll be footing the bill."

20

"They're gone," Jim Court reported that next morning when he opened the door of the old saddlery and stepped inside. "Knew that damned hasp wouldn't be enough to hold them."

Thompson fired a match with his thumbnail, puffed his cigar into life. They had spent an enjoyable night at Mrs. Letty's place, as they learned it was called, had an early breakfast, and gone then to see about their prisoners.

"It sure wasn't," the detective agreed indifferently. "Means we'll have to get busy, dig them out."

Court was studying Thompson intently. "This's what you was figuring on all the time, ain't it?"

The range detective made an offhand gesture. "Don't see as that matters for much now. What we got to do is find them prisoners. Sure hate losing them."

"You think they're still in town?"

"Sure. Seen the horses was still there

where we picketed them when we came by, didn't you?"

The young deputy fell silent for a time. Then, "Well, where do we start the looking?"

"Right here," Thompson said, and raking together a pile of paper, bits of wood, and other trash with a booted foot, he pushed it against a wall of the old saddle shop, struck a match, and dropped it into the tinder-dry accumulation.

"What —" Court blurted in alarm, and leaped forward.

Thompson brushed him back. "You know a better way to drive the rats out of a place than by setting it on fire?" he asked, mildly, and pulled away as the flames began to greedily lick at the dry wood.

"But here — this place! Ain't no sense burning it down because they ain't in it," the deputy protested. "And with that morning breeze, the fire's liable to spread."

"Yeh, expect it will," the range detective said blandly.

The fire was gaining rapidly and the building was filling with smoke. Thompson backed toward the doorway.

"We best step outside — sort of let things happen," he said, and then, when they were again in the street, added, "Your gun loaded?"

Court drew his pistol, spun the cylinder. "All six holes."

"Fine. You'll likely be using it. Let's drop around behind the place and walk up to the end of the street, get things to going there."

"What things?" the deputy wondered, following the detective around to the now furiously blazing structure. Flames were shooting up into the sky and glowing embers were beginning to float about in the light wind.

"We're setting fire to everything here," Thompson replied in a calm voice, turning into the alley. "Aim to clean out the place."

Yells were now coming from the street as persons in the saloons and other buildings, suddenly aware of the mounting conflagration, were rushing into the open.

"You figuring on burning down the whole town?" Court asked in an incredulous voice.

Thompson nodded, halted at the back of the next structure in line, one that had also been abandoned.

"Been a holing-up place for outlaws long enough. Aim to change that," the range detective said. Glancing through the glassless window in the rear of the building, he grunted in satisfaction and, lighting another match, dropped it inside. "Saddle tramps been using this one for a hotel. Lot of paper and shavings on the floor. Ought to catch quick."

He moved on, seemingly oblivious to the shouts and confusion raging in the street on the opposite side of the structure. Suddenly he halted, faced Jim Court.

"Deputy, if you ain't got the sand for this, it'll be all right. Go wait for me with the horses. I'll be along in a couple hours or so."

Court, eyeing the flames now spouting from a gaping window of the second building, shook his head. "No, reckon not, Marshal. I'll trail along with you."

Thompson smiled faintly. "Get out your matches then, son. I don't want nothing but ashes left around here when we ride out."

They continued along the alley, putting the torch to several small shacks and sheds, another vacant store building, and then came to the end of the street. They paused there, looked back. Starting with the saddlery, their side of the street all the way to its end was a roaring wall of flame. Above the town a thick layer of smoke hung, and the air was filled with sparks, drifting embers, and the shouts of people, hurrying back and forth, as they endeavored to check the spreading fire. Thompson seemed unaware of the frantic activity. He pointed to the structure on the opposite side of the street. It was the livery stable.

"Going to be horses in there," he said. "Got to turn them loose first."

Without waiting for any comment from the young deputy, he broke out into the street and, ignoring the milling crowd farther down, crossed over. Entering the stable, he started down the runway, glancing into each stall.

Jim Court overtook him and together they released the half-dozen or so animals that were in the broad, low-roofed building, drove them out the rear and onto the grassy flat beyond. Doubling back, Thompson took a lantern from a nail near the stable's entrance, smashed it against an inner wall. Court lit a match and tossed it into the spilled oil, and as flames shot up instantaneously, he followed the range detective out into the street.

Structures on below the saddle shop were now burning, the drifting sparks having found purchase on their sun-bleached roofs and walls. Thompson, halting at the side of the first building south of the stable, a small saloon, looked about for something with which to set it aflame.

Finding nothing, he stepped through the doorway of the narrow structure, deserted at the moment as were all other establishments, picked up a lamp, and dashing it to the floor, flipped a match into the resulting pool of coal oil. Moving hastily to escape the explosion of flame, he rejoined the deputy.

The crackling of the fires was almost deafening and the heavy pall of smoke had thickened even more and was beginning to drift slowly toward the east. Half of Boston's buildings were burning wildly and unchecked as the crowd in the street, with no water available other than the few barrels hauled in, were powerless to check the fires.

"We've been spotted!" Court shouted above the heat-filled din, and pointed to the lower end of the town.

A half-dozen men had broken clear of the knot of people, were advancing. Thompson spat his cigar butt into the dust, squinted through the haze at the shoulder to shoulder line.

"That'll be Red and some of his bunch," he said. "Was wondering when they'd wise up and start looking for us."

Pivoting, he stepped to the edge of the street, halted at the corner of the building next in the row below the now-raging saloon. The heat was intense and sparks were dropping all around him, some lodging on his clothing. He seemed not to notice.

"Best you keep behind me," he said to Court, and once again put his attention on the approaching outlaws.

They were less than fifty yards distant. Through narrowed eyes smarting from the pungent smoke, the range detective considered them. Red King . . . Art Lea . . . Webb Durham . . . Al Lester . . . two he didn't recognize.

"There's our horse-stealing friend, Lester," Bill said to the deputy. "Gone and teamed up with King. Now, he's an escaped prisoner. You feel like it, put a bullet in him."

Thompson didn't wait for any reply from Jim Court. Abruptly, pistol in hand, he stepped away from the wall of the building. A yell went up from one of the six outlaws and all came to a stop. Immediately Thompson's gun began to blast, the reports coming so fast they blended into a continuous roll.

Two of the outlaws, King and Durham, staggered, went down. Lea managed to drag out his weapon, trigger a hurried shot. It was wild — and his last. He buckled as one of the range detective's bullets drove into him. Lester was also falling, victim of Jim Court's aim, but the two unrecognized men were still on their feet, unhit and seemingly paralyzed, unable to move. Abruptly both regained their presence of mind and, wheeling, headed back down the smoke-filled street at a hard run.

Thompson, reloading his near-empty pistol, watched them disappear into the restless crowd. Nearby, Court, also rodding the empties from the cylinder of his weapon and shoving in fresh cartridges, let his gaze rest on the figures of the outlaws sprawled in the dust.

"We going after the rest of them?" he asked, his voice taut. "I reckon we ought to do the job up right."

Thompson, gun again ready and back in its holster, turned his soot-streaked face to the younger man. "You growed up fast, Deputy," he said with a slow smile. "But we don't need to be going after them — they'll be looking for us. Best we get on with the burning."

Court nodded and then pointed to the rear of the building. Flames were licking along the edge of the roof. "This'n is already going up. Sparks from the saloon must've fell on it."

"Good. Saves us the trouble," the detective said laconically, and moved on. Just past the structure he hesitated, glanced down the street, turned into the passageway lying between it and its neighbor, and continued on for the alley behind it.

"Plumb foolish staying out there in the open," he said. "Some two-bit jasper in that crowd could take a potshot at us and we'd never know who he was. One thing a man needs to learn if he's aiming to be a lawman is when it's time to be brave and when it's time to use his common sense."

They used trash piled against the next store building to set it afire and came then to the rear of the Palace saloon. Thompson, not slowing, stepped up to the back door, jerked it open, and entered.

There was no one present, and looking on through the clouded windows in the front, he could see the crowd still milling uselessly about as they watched the town being steadily consumed by the flames. He watched for a moment and then, crossing to the near wall, lifted a lamp from its bracket, as he'd done previously, and threw it to the floor.

The lamp failed to break, and stepping up to it, he smashed it under foot. Jim Court was close by, and before he could strike a match, the deputy had fired one of his own and was tossing it into the spreading oil. It caught instantly and both men wheeled at once and retreated to the alley.

The general store, a vacant shack, the saloon where they had the night before slaked their thirsts, and Mrs. Letty's place were all that remained untouched by fire on that side of the street.

The storekeeper, accepting the inevitable and aided by several friends, was carrying out his more-cherished belongings and piling them into a wagon drawn up in front of his establishment. Two men were standing by the nervous horses which appeared ready to bolt at any moment as the crackling flames drew nearer.

Yells went up suddenly as the fire inside the Palace made itself known, and a small party broke clear of the crowd and dashed into the structure hopeful, apparently, of saving some of their possessions. Elsewhere along the street a half-dozen men, with guns drawn, were making their way toward its upper end as they began a search for the cause of the holocaust. Thompson pointed at them, now halted and viewing the bodies of Red King and his friends.

"Looking for us," he said, studying the group thoughtfully as if weighing the need to oblige them. His shoulders moved indifferently. "We'll just let them keep on looking."

Court was silent for a time, listening to the confusion of sounds that gripped the heat and smoke-enveloped settlement.

Then, "You figure there's any need bothering with the store?" he asked in a casual, matter-of-fact way. He had adjusted to the job they were doing, was evidently seeing it much as if it were an ordinary, everyday occurrence rather than the complete destruction of a town.

Thompson considered, reached for a cigar, and wedged it between his teeth. "No use. It's going to catch from the Palace. We leave it be so that counter-jumper'll have time to haul out all he aims to."

"What about the saloon, the one where we done our drinking?"

"Expect there'll be some trash out back. Can drop a match in it, start it going — then we'd best see to the horses. Looks like that shack near where we left them's burning."

"That'll be the last one — 'cepting Mrs. Letty's."

Again Bill Thompson fell silent. "We'll leave it be," he said finally. "Maybe it'll get missed — all depending on how good Mrs. Letty's luck is."

21

Mrs. Letty's luck was all bad. Despite the fact that her house was somewhat removed from other structures in the town, dry grass and dead weeds caught fire, and fanned by the breeze coming from the high hills to the north, the flames raced to meet and consume the ornate residence in which she and her girls, as she termed them, provided recreation for the cowhands and other men who came to visit.

Halted on a rise well away from the settlement, Bill Thompson and Deputy Jim Court looked back on the results of their handiwork. Mrs. Letty's place was a square mass of surging, leaping flames; and nearby, a black smear of smoking, smoldering embers out of which reared an occasional solitary post or the charred remnants of what had once been a wall, was all that remained of Boston.

"Feel kind of sorrowful looking back at the place," Court said. "It's sure dead now."

"Expect it'll stay that way, too," Thomp-

son said, the inevitable cigar clamped between his teeth. "No need for anybody re-
building there."

"Need for the town was gone a long time
ago when all the farmers went busted. Too
bad about the decent folks that was still
living there, though."

"Was mighty few of them, if any."

"Yeh, most of them had already move on.
Ranchers around here ought to be plenty
happy over what we've done. They been bel-
lyaching about the place ever since I can remember."

The range detective nodded. "About the
only ones that ain't going to appreciate it are
the cowhands that've been hanging around
the saloons and calling on Mrs. Letty's girls."

The deputy laughed. Then, "You have
doing this in your mind all the time? Was it
why we went there instead of riding straight
on to La Junta?"

"Heard McBride, or maybe it was somebody else, complaining about the town,
saying it weren't nothing but a hideout for
outlaws. Seen that it was the day I dropped
by and had myself a look. The association
hired me to clean out such trash, and I figured this'd be a good time to do it. Sort of
got an old score settled up while I was doing
it, too."

"That bunch we shot it out with in the street?"

Thompson merely grunted, his small eyes reaching across the distance to Mrs. Letty's. The last of the house, the south wall, was falling. He could see a dozen or so persons standing nearby looking on, slim, upright blurs in the dense haze. Elsewhere, in the center of what had been the town, others were moving about among the cooling ruins as if searching for lost possessions.

"Could be a mite hard explaining all this to the association — especially losing them horse thieves."

"Only one," the detective corrected. "Far as doing any explaining, they can like it or they can kiss my hind end. We broke up a nest of bank robbers, killers, rustlers, and the like — and that's what I was hired to do."

"But Boston was over the line — in Colorado."

Thompson shrugged. "That make a difference? An outlaw's an outlaw — don't make a damn where he is."

"Could be some trouble with the Colorado law."

"Maybe, but I'm laying odds they'll be as glad to be rid of that place as the ranchers," the detective said, and cutting his horse about, struck for the Strip.

It was early afternoon when they reached the line shack. Waiting for them, besides Frank Lacey, were Amos Lindeman, McBride, and Charlie Gere. Thompson, dismounting at the hitchrack, bobbed slightly to each and silently moved past them to the shack. Entering, he poured himself a cup of coffee and spooned out a plate of warm beans and sowbelly to satisfy his hunger.

Out in the yard Jim Court had been halted by the ranchers and was being questioned by them. The young deputy, his clothing bearing scorch marks from falling sparks and embers, appeared to be giving them a full accounting of their activities.

Thompson, finishing off the beans and meat and nursing the coffee, returned to the doorway and leaned up against the frame. His stolid face was still streaked with soot and his shirt and hat also showed damage from the fires.

Waiting until the deputy had finished his report, the detective said, "Since you was already waiting here for us, I take it you'd already heard."

The ranchers turned to him. Lindeman said, "Was a couple of my men close by when it all started — so they say. Expect the truth is they was both laying up with some

201

women in that bawdy house. They hung around till they saw what was going on, then rode out. Come across a couple other of my boys on the range, told them. It was them that brought the word to me."

"Jim tells us that you burned the place to the ground," McBride said.

"Was what I intended to do."

The rancher nodded, rubbed at his jaw. His features were stiff, solemn. "You realize, Marshal, there could be some trouble over this. Boston wasn't in the Panhandle — was in Colorado, out of your territory."

The range detective finished off his coffee. "Anybody complains tell them to talk to me," he said indifferently.

"Ain't none of us complaining!" Gere said with a broad grin. "Not by a damn sight! About the best thing that could happen to us!"

"That's a fact," Lindeman said. "You're doing that on top of cleaning up the range for us the way you have's going to serve as a notice to all rustlers and other outlaws that there ain't no room for them around here any longer."

"Don't get me wrong," McBride said. "I'm mighty happy about it — just wondering about the legal side of it."

"Oh, the hell with the legal side, John!"

Gere declared. "Who's going to do any hollering? Them owlhoots he burned out? Property wasn't theirs in the first place; either they'd moved in and took over a vacant building or maybe even had scared off the rightful owner. They ain't about to do any squawking.

"And if somebody shows up claiming damages, I say we can afford to pay them off. That damned hellhole has cost us all plenty in the last few years with them saloons and that bunch of women being real handy like they was. My crew's spent about half the time they're supposed to be on the job, there."

"Same here," Lindeman said. "Expect Davidson and Clete Potter and all the rest of the association will agree."

"There won't be any hollering done," Thompson said from the doorway, "but if there is, I'll answer up to it. Was my doing and I'll stand by it."

"Appreciate that, Marshal," McBride said, "but you're working for us and we feel responsible for what you do."

"That ain't necessary. I'm working for myself, too, and things I do when I'm on my own, I reckon you'd best overlook. That way you won't need to lose no sleep."

Charlie Gere nodded. "As good a way as

any to look at it but, nevertheless, we're behind you no matter what you do. Want you to know that. You've done for us what nobody else's ever been able to do — and that's counting not only our own selves but outside lawmen that we've called in."

"Not that any of them even tried," Lindeman added. "Always the same story — no-man's-land and they didn't have the authority to act."

Thompson pivoted abruptly, dropped back into the shack, and refilled his cup. He was totally disinterested in what was being said; the deed had been done, an act that, in his judgment, was warranted, and whether anyone else felt it was justified did not concern him.

Retracing his steps to the doorway, he put his attention on Frank Lacey, standing a bit apart from the ranchers now in conversation among themselves.

"Anybody send word they was having trouble?"

The deputy nodded, moved up. "Cowhand of Potter's rode in, said there was a bunch building a lean-to down in the brakes — lower end of Clete's range."

"Squatters or drifters?"

"He didn't say."

Thompson sipped thoughtfully at his

coffee. "Reckon we'd best drop by there to-morrow. Anybody else?"

"Nope."

"Way I see it, you about got every jaybird hunting for a place to roost scared of trying the Strip," Gere said, coming in on the comments. "Which is sure what we been wanting."

The detective drained his cup, tossed it back onto the table behind him. "Could be crowing a mite too soon. I'll do a bit of riding, have a look at the range — all of it. When I get done with that, then maybe you can all start feeling the job's been done." He shifted his attention to Jim Court. "You be ready to ride in the morning, Deputy?"

Court grinned. "Sure. Anytime you say."

"Go for you, too," Thompson said, looking at Lacey.

The older deputy's lips also cracked into a smile, one of relief. He apparently had expected to be excluded. "Yes, sir, Marshal. Whenever you want."

"Then, come first light, we'll head out. Probably be gone a few days, so bring along enough grub."

22

Bill Thompson and his deputies found the range clear. They spent a number of days crisscrossing the lengthy panhandle, encountered no one that wasn't entitled to be there. It hadn't taken long for word to spread that the Strip, under the cold eye of the feared Regulator, now offered no safe retreat for outlaws on the dodge, and that squatters were equally unwelcome. The fiery demise of Boston further emphasized the point.

With the knowledge of that fact, a restlessness came to the squat, broad-faced range detective, and only a few short weeks after he had ridden into McBride's yard and assumed the task for which he had been summoned, he again presented himself to the rancher. As usual Jim Court and Frank Lacey were with him.

"Job's done," he said in his blunt, sparse manner. "Like to draw my pay."

McBride studied him for several moments. Then, "You figure the deputies can handle it now?"

"They won't have no trouble. Range is clean, they can easy keep it that way."

The rancher glanced to Lacey and Court. "That how you see it?"

"Sure is," the older deputy assured him. "Big job was rousting the squatters and rustlers off the land, and getting the word out that it ain't healthy for any of their likes around here. Jim and me can keep it that way."

McBride made no comment, wheeled, and entered the house. He returned shortly, an envelope thick with currency in his hand, and passed it to the detective.

"You'll find what we agreed on in there, along with a little bonus," he said.

Bill folded the envelope, tucked it inside his shirt. McBride grinned.

"Ain't you going to count it?"

The detective shrugged, glanced at the sky to the north. Dingy gray clouds were beginning to pile up on the ragged horizon, and there was the distinct smell of winter in the air.

"I don't figure you'd cheat me," he said finally. "Obliged to you for the extra."

"Welcome. Which way you heading?"

"North, for a ways. There's a fellow I know working on the JX Ranch, near Higbee. Name's Jack Egan. Aim to drop by there, say my howdies, then go on back to Texas."

"You be around the JX for a spell, just in case somebody asks for you?"

"Yeh, reckon I will."

The rancher extended his hand. "Well, I guess this is so long then, Marshal. Want you to know me and the association are plenty grateful for what you've done."

"What you paid me for," Thompson said, turning to the deputies. Solemnly shaking their hands, he murmured, "Luck," and crossing to his buckskin, mounted and rode out of the yard.

Thompson, taking his ease in the bunk-house of the JX Ranch, considered his old friend thoughtfully. They had served in the war together, done a bit of aimless wandering a time later when the fracas was all over, and then separated, Egan heading north to hunt for gold in Colorado, Bill settling down in Texas to try his hand at raising cattle.

"Was a mite surprised to hear you was working on a ranch," he said. "Figured you'd be a rich man owning half the country by now."

"Just wasn't no good at digging in the ground," Egan, a thin, leathery man in his late forties, said, pausing to glance at two other men in the dimly lit room. Sitting at the table ordinarily used by the help for poker playing, they were bickering over some matter that was in contention between them. "Didn't have no luck at it, either."

"Ought to beat fence riding —"

"If you mean working for myself, I expect it does, only the pay ain't as regular. Dammit, Curly, why don't you and Norm go outside and do your arguing? Can't talk for all your yammering."

"This here's a free country," the curly-haired cowpuncher snapped, "and if me and Rosston want to do some arguing, why, I reckon we'll do it. Maybe you and your friend there ought to go outside if we're bothering you."

Egan shrugged, brought his attention back to Thompson. "Them two've been pals a long time," he said in a low voice. "But lately something's come up that sure's sticking crossways in their craws. I'm thinking we're about to see the busting up of a friendship."

Thompson considered the two cowhands. Both were young, had just come in off the range, and were still wearing their batwing chaps. Hard words were passing between them as they came through the doorway and there had been no letup.

"You know what it's all about?"

"Nope. It's their business, and they ain't said, so nobody's asked."

"Too bad," the range detective commented. "Good friends are a bit hard to come by these days."

"For sure. You say you're heading back to Texas?"

Bill nodded. "Aim to go down around San Antone, lay around there for the winter. Maybe even go over into Mexico. Sort of feel like taking it easy for a spell."

"Sounds real nice. Expect you've earned it after doing the job you done on the Strip."

"Wasn't no different from any other job. Why don't you come along with me? You ain't doing nothing much here to keep you, and I got money enough for both of us."

Egan shifted on his chair, his lean features drawn into a frown. "Now, dammit, Bill, I ain't no charity case! I got a little cash salted away in my poke, but what you're saying does sound pretty good. Getting so I can't take these here cold winters so good anymore, and —"

Egan broke off abruptly as Curly and Norm Rosston sprang to their feet, knocking over their chairs in the process. Curly, his mouth working angrily, dropped a hand to the pistol on his hip.

"By God, I ain't taking that from no-body!"

"Hold on now, boys," Thompson said, rising and stepping in front of Rosston. "Whatever you're arguing about can't be serious enough to call for guns."

"Keep out of this, mister," Rosston said through clenched teeth. "If he wants a shooting, he's sure as hell's going to get it!"

The detective shook his head. "From what Jack tells me you two've been friends for a long time. Plain foolish to let all that go to waste over something that like as not ain't nothing more than a mix up."

Rosston eased off but continued to glare at Curly from across the table. "Yeh, guess maybe it is."

"What started it, anyway? Could be I can sort of act like a judge, help you straighten it out."

Rosston's shoulders stirred. "Was only something I said he didn't cotton to. Truth is, I didn't mean it the way he took it."

Curly bristled. "Goddamn words was plain enough!"

"Was you twisting them around and making them mean something they didn't that started the trouble!" Rosston shot back.

"Just back up, both of you," Thompson said sternly. "Can see this is just a misunderstanding and all you need to do is set down, calmlike, and talk it over. But you first need cooling off. Curly, you go on out the front door there with Egan; I'll take Rosston through the back. In ten or fifteen minutes we'll get together in here again and clear this up. Fair enough?"

Curly nodded, pivoted, and started for the entrance to the bunkhouse. Thompson, pushing Norm Rosston before him, moved toward the rear of the narrow building.

"The hell with it — I'm done talking!" Curly shouted unexpectedly, and whipping out his pistol, spun and fired.

The bullet struck Thompson — not its intended victim — in the head just as he wheeled. It killed him instantly.

Thus William Thompson, the dreaded Regulator, the peerless gunmaster and range detective who had faced and shot it out with a dozen or more of the most desperate outlaws, died quickly and quite by accident.

Author's Note

I wish to extend my sincere appreciation to the many persons residing in the area once ridden by Bill Thompson, the famed Regulator, who graciously granted me interviews and related whatever information they possessed concerning the man. Admittedly, none of them knew Thompson personally, he having met his curious and atypical death in the early 1890s, but many were able to recall the stories told to them by their elders, and it was upon those anecdotes and the facts available that this account was based.

To the several libraries in New Mexico and Colorado, I also owe thanks, along with an expression of gratitude to the Otero County Clerk's office, La Junta, Colorado; Bent County Clerk's office, Las Animas, Colorado; Vital Records Division, Denver, Colorado; and to Ed Bartholomew of Fort Davis, Texas.

The employees of Thorndike Press hope you have enjoyed this Large Print book. All our Thorndike and Wheeler Large Print titles are designed for easy reading, and all our books are made to last. Other Thorndike Press Large Print books are available at your library, through selected bookstores, or directly from us.

For information about titles, please call:

(800) 223-1244

or visit our Web site at:

www.gale.com/thorndike
www.gale.com/wheeler

To share your comments, please write:

Publisher
Thorndike Press
295 Kennedy Memorial Drive
Waterville, ME 04901